THE
TRANSPOSED
HEADS

A
LEGEND
OF
INDIA

*Translated
from
the
German
by
H. T.
Lowe–Porter*

THE

TRANSPOSED

HEADS

A

LEGEND

OF

INDIA

BY

THOMAS

MANN

NEW
YORK
VINTAGE
BOOKS

1959

PUBLISHED BY VINTAGE BOOKS, INC.

Reprinted by arrangement with ALFRED A. KNOPF, INC.

FIRST VINTAGE EDITION

To
Heinrich
Zimmer
the
great
Indian
scholar
Returned
with
thanks

TRANSPOSED
HEADS

A
LEGEND
OF
INDIA

The story of Sita of the beautiful hips, daughter of the cattle-breeder Sumantra of the warrior caste, and of her two husbands (if one may put it like that) is so sanguinary, so amazing to the senses, that it makes the greatest demands on the hearer's strength of mind and his power to resist the gruesome guiles of Maya. It would be well for the listener to take pattern from the fortitude of the teller, for it requires, if anything, more courage to tell such a tale than to hear it. But here it is, from first to last, just as it fell out:

At the time when memory mounted in the mind of man, as the vessel of sacrifice slowly fills up from the bottom with drink or with blood; when the womb of stern patriarchal piety opened to the seed of the primeval past, nostalgia for the Mother reinvested with new shudderings the ancient images and swelled the number of pilgrims thronging in the spring to the shrines of the great World-Nurse; at such a time it was that two youths, little different in age and caste, but very unlike in body, were vowed to friendship. The younger was named Nanda, the somewhat elder Shridaman. The first was eighteen years old, the second already one-and-twenty; both, each on his proper day, had been girt with the sacred cord and received into the company of the twice-born. Their homes were in the temple village called Welfare of Cows, which had been settled in time past on a sign from the gods in its

place in the land of Kosala. It was surrounded by a
cactus hedge and a wooden wall; its gates, facing
the four points of the compass, had been blessed
by a wandering wise man and familiar of the goddess Speech—who uttered no incorrect word, and
had been given to eat in the village—with the blessing that its door-posts and lintels should drop fat-
ness and honey.

The friendship between the two youths was
based on the diversity in their I- and my-feelings,
those of the one yearning towards those of the
other. Incorporation, that is, makes for isolation,
isolation for difference; difference makes for comparisons, comparisons give rise to uneasiness, uneasiness to wonderment, wonderment tends to admiration; and finally admiration turns to a yearning
for mutual exchange and unity. *Etad vai tad.* This
is that. And the doctrine applies especially in youth,
when the clay of life is still soft and the I- and my-
feelings not yet hardened into the division of the
single personality.

Young Shridaman was a merchant, and the son
of a merchant; Nanda, on the other hand, both a
smith and a cowherd, for his father Garga not only
kept cattle on the meadow and in the byre, but
also plied the hammer and fanned the fire with a
bird's wing. As for Shridaman's sire, Bhavabhuti
by name, he traced his line on the male side from
a Brahman stock versed in the Vedas, which Garga
and his son were far from doing. Still, they were
no Sudras, and although somewhat goat-nosed,
were quite distinctly members of human society.
Anyhow, for Shridaman, and even for Bhavabhuti,

the Brahman way of life was only a memory, for Bhavabhuti's father had deliberately abandoned it at the stage of householder, which follows that of student, and never gone on to be either forest hermit or ascetic to the end of his days. He had scorned to live only on gifts from pious respecters of his knowledge of the Vedas, perhaps he had not been content with these; for he had opened up a good business in mull, silk and calico, camphor and sandalwood. And his son in his turn, though begotten for the service of the gods, had become a vanija or merchant in the village of Welfare of Cows, and Bhavabhuti's son Shridaman followed in his father's footsteps, after having previously devoted some years to grammar and the elements of astronomy and ontology, under the supervision of a guru or spiritual preceptor.

Not so Nanda, son of Garga. His karma was otherwise; and never, by either tradition or inheritance, had he had to do with things of the mind. No, he was just as he was, a son of the people, simple and blithe, a Krishna-manifestation, dark of skin and hair; he even had the "lucky-calf" lock on his breast. His work as a smith had made powerful his arms; that as a shepherd had been further an advantage, for he had a well set-up body, which he loved to rub with mustard oil and drape with gold ornaments and chains of wild flowers. There was harmony between it and the pleasant beardless face, despite the rather thick lips and the suggestion of a goat-nose; even these were attractive in their way, and his black eyes almost always wore a laugh.

Shridaman very much liked all this, comparing it with himself, who was several shades lighter in both head and limbs, with a face too quite otherwise shaped. The ridge of his nose was thin as a blade; eyes he had, soft of pupil and lid, and on his cheeks a soft fan-shaped beard. Soft too were his limbs, not moulded by exercise as cowherd and smith, even rather Brahman-like, as well as clerkly, with a rather soft, narrow breast and some fat on the little belly, but otherwise flawless, with fine knee-joints and feet. It was a body proper to serve as adjunct and appendage to a noble and knowledgeable headpiece, that was of course head and front of the whole, whereas with the whole Nanda the body was, so to speak, the main thing, and the head merely a pleasing appendage. All in all the two were like Siva in his double manifestation, lying sometimes as dead, a bearded ascetic, at the feet of the goddess, but sometimes erect, a figure in the bloom of youth, stretching his young limbs as he turns towards her.

But after all they were not one like Siva, who is life and death, world and eternity in the Mother, but manifested as two entities here below; thus they were to each other like images. The my-feeling of each was tired of itself, and though each was aware that after all everything consists of what it has not got, yet on account of their very differences they intrigued each other. The fine-lipped, soft-bearded Shridaman found pleasure in the rude primeval Krishna-nature of the thick-lipped Nanda; while he, partly flattered, but partly and even more, because he felt impressed by Shridaman's light complexion, his noble headpiece and correct diction—which, of course, was from the beginning of things inseparable from wisdom and philosophy, and one with these—on his side knew nothing more lovely than intercourse with Shridaman; thus it was they became fast friends. Certainly in the inclination of each for the other some slight humour inhered; Nanda privately made fun of Shridaman's fair fatness, his thin nose and punctilious speech. Shridaman, on the other hand, smiled at Nanda's goat-nose and rustic simplicity. This sort of private criticism is a common feature of the uneasiness born of comparison; it is a tribute to the I- and my-feeling, and does no least violence to the Maya longing born of the same.

Well, then, it came about that in the lovely springtime, when the air was full of the noise of birds, Nanda and Shridaman took a walking-tour together through the country, each on his own occasions. Nanda had from his father Garga the task of buying a certain quantity of black ore from a community of lowly folk, clad only in reed aprons, who were skilful smelters and with whom Nanda knew how to talk. These folk dwelt in mud huts some days' journey from the friends' village, and nearer the town of Kurukshetra, which in its turn was somewhat north of the thickly populated Indra-prastha, on the river Jumna. Here Shridaman's errand lay, with a business friend of the family, him-self a Brahman who had not got further than the stage of householder. With this man Shridaman was to barter to the best advantage some fine-coloured cloths woven by the village women at home, for some rice-mallets and a particularly practical kind of firewood, of which there was need at Welfare of Cows.

They had travelled a day and a half, on peopled highways and through empty woods and wastes, each bearing his fardel on his back: Nanda a box of betel-nuts, cowrie-shells, and alta-red on bast paper to redden the soles of the feet, for with these he thought to pay the lowly folk for their ore; Shrida-man his cloths sewed up in a doeskin. Nanda out of sheer friendliness carried the other's burden too, from time to time. They came now to a bathing-place, sacred to Kali, the All-Embracing, Mother of the worlds and of all beings, who is the dream-drunkenness of Vishnu. It lay on the stream Goldfly, which rushes, like a colt let loose, out of the mountain's womb, to moderate its flow and unite at a holy place with the river Jumna; that in its turn issuing, at a place yet more holy, into the eternal Ganges. But the Ganges flows by its many mouths into the sea. Many bathing-places of high repute, which cleanse all defilement, where one drawing up the water of life and plunging into its bosom may receive new birth—many such stand on the banks and mouths of the Ganges, and at the junction of other rivers with the terrestrial Milky Way, as at the point where Goldfly, little daughter of the snows, joins with the Jumna. Everywhere in this region, in short, such shrines and sites of purification abound, convenient to all for sacrifice and communion. They are provided with consecrated stairs, so that the pious need not plump awkwardly and irreligiously through reed and lotus into the water, but may step down in dignity to drink and to lave themselves.

Now, this bathing-place the friends had hit on was not one of the larger ones, full of offerings, renowned for its miracles, and thronged by noble and simple, though of course at different hours. No, it was a quiet, retired little spot, not at a meeting of rivers, just somewhere on the river-bank, which at that point climbed above the bed of the Goldfly. On top of the bank stood the little temple, built simply of wood and already somewhat rickety though carved in pleasing designs. It was the temple of the Mistress of all desires and joys, with a bulbous tower above the cella. The steps leading to the spring were wooden too and rather broken, yet good enough for a dignified descent.

The youths expressed their pleasure at having hit on this spot, which gave them opportunity for worship, refreshment and rest in the shade. It was already very hot at midday; the heavy summer threatened untimely, and at the sides of the little temple the growth of mangoes, teak and kadamba trees, magnolias, tamarisks, and tala palms made shelter where it would be good to rest and breakfast. The friends first performed their religious duties, as well as circumstances permitted. There was no priest from whom to purchase oil or clarified butter to anoint the stone linga images on the little terrace before the temple. They found a ladle, scooped up water from the river, and did their pious service, murmuring the appropriate words. Then they descended, cupping their hands, into the green riverbed; drank, poured the ritual water, dipped, and gave thanks. Out of pure enjoyment they stopped in the water a little longer than the spiritually requisite time; then, feeling in all their limbs the blessing of purification, returned to the resting-place they had selected under the trees.

Here like brothers they shared their bite, though one had no different from the other, and each might have eaten his own. When Nanda broke a barley cake, he handed half of it to Shridaman saying: "There, old fellow." Shridaman, dividing a piece of fruit, gave half to Nanda with the same words. Shridaman sat to eat, sideways to his food, knees and feet together, in the grass that was here still green and unsinged. Nanda squatted rustically with his knees up and feet in front of him, as one cannot long sit without being born to it. They took up these attitudes unconsciously and without thought; if they had paid heed to the manner of their sitting, Shridaman, out of sheer inclination to the primitive, would have sat with his knees up and Nanda put himself sideways in the contrary desire. He wore a little cap on his sleek black hair, still wet from the bath; a loincloth of white cotton cloth, rings on his upper arms, and round his neck a necklace of stone-pearls held together with gold bands. Through it one could see the "lucky-calf" lock on his breast. Shridaman had a white cloth wound around his head and wore his white cotton short-sleeved smock falling over his full draped apron, that hung like trousers. In the neck-opening of the smock there showed an amulet-pouch on a thin chain. Both wore the sign of their faith painted in mineral-white on their foreheads.

When they had eaten they put aside the remnants and talked. It was so delightful here that princes and kings could not have fared better. Between the tall stems of calamus and bamboo, whose foliage and clusters of blossoms made a light rustling, they could see the pool and the lower steps going down to it. Clinging water-plants made charming garlands from bough to bough. The chirping and trilling of unseen birds mingled with the humming of insects that darted to and fro returning ever and anon to the flowering grasses. The cool freshness and warm breath of all these plants perfumed the air; there was the headiness of the jasmine, the peculiar scent of the tala-fruit; sandalwood and mustard oil—Nanda had anointed himself with this last after the ritual of the bath.

"Here we seem to be beyond the six waves of hunger and thirst, age and death, suffering and illusion," said Shridaman. "It is extraordinarily peaceful. It is as though we were moved from the restless whirl of life and placed in its motionless centre where we can draw a long breath. Hark! How cosy and hushed it is here! I use the word 'hushed' because we say hush when we want to listen; and listening can only properly be done where there is a hush. It lets us listen to everything in it which is not entirely still, so that the stillness speaks as in a dream and we hear it too as though we were dreaming."

"It is verily true as thy word sayeth," responded Nanda. "In the noise of the market-place one does not listen, that is only done where there is a hush that even so holds this and that to listen to. Quite soundless, filled with silence, is only Nirvana, and so you could never call it hushed, nor yet cosy."

"No," answered Shridaman, and could not help laughing. "It has probably not occurred to anyone to call Nirvana hushed, and certainly not cosy; yet you do it, in a sort of way, if only by negation, when you say that one cannot do it; and so you find out the funniest of all the negations—for only so can Nirvana be spoken of, of course—that could ever be uttered about it. You do say such shrewd things sometimes, if I may use the word 'shrewd' about something which is at once absurd and perfectly correct. I like it very much, sometimes it makes my diaphragm contract suddenly, almost like a sob.

Thus we see how close together are laughing and weeping; so that it is an illusion to make any distinction between pleasure and pain, and like the one and hate the other, when, after all, both can be called good and both bad. But there is a combination of laughter and tears which one can most readily assent to and call good among all things that move us in life. We have a word for it, we call it touching; it has to do with sympathy on the cheerful side, and is just what makes the contraction of my diaphragm so much like a sob. And it is that that hurts me about your shrewdness."

"But why does it hurt you?" Nanda asked.

"Because after all you are actually a child of Samsara and thus completely taken up with life," answered Shridaman; "you do not belong among the souls who feel the need to emerge above the frightful ocean of laughing and weeping as lotus flowers rise above the surface of the stream and open their cups to the sky. You are perfectly at home in the depths, where such a complex profusion and variety of shapes and forms exist. You are well off, and that is why one feels good at the sight of you. Then you suddenly get the idea in your head to meddle with Nirvana and talk about its negative condition and how it cannot be called hushed nor cosy, and all that is funny enough to make one weep, or, to use the word made on purpose, it is touching, because it makes me grieve for that well-being of yours that is so good to see."

"But listen to me," countered Nanda. "I don't understand. You might be sorry I am so taken up with Samsara and cannot go in for being a lotus. That is all right. But to be hurt because I try to take an interest in Nirvana, as well as I can—that might not be so good. You have hurt me too, let me tell you."

"And in what way then do I in my turn hurt you?" Shridaman asked.

"Because you have read the Vedas and learned about the nature of being," replied Nanda, "but even so you are more easily blinded by Samsara than people who have not. That is what really tickles me; it gives me, as you say, a feeling of sympathy on the cheerful side. It is more or less hushed in this spot where we are; so you let yourself go on about being beyond the six waves of hunger and thirst, and think you are in life's resting centre. And yet all the hush, and all the things you can listen to in it, are just a sign that there is a lot going on and your notions about peace and quiet are just notions. The birds coo because they are making love; all these bees and bugs and cockchafers are darting about in search of food; the grass is alive with sounds of life-and-death struggles we cannot hear. The very vines so tenderly embracing the trees would like to strangle them to take their sap and air to batten on. And there you have the true knowledge of life."

"I know it well," Shridaman said, "I do not blind myself to it, or at least only for the moment and because I want to. For there is not only the truth and knowledge of the understanding, but also the insight of the human heart, which sees as in an allegory and knows how to read the handwriting of all phenomena, not only in its first and simple sense but also in its second and higher one, using it as means whereby to look through at the pure and spiritual. How will you arrive at a perception of peace, and feel the joy of a cessation from conflict, unless you have a Maya-image to give you a hold on it—though in itself a Maya-image is by no means peace and joy! It is granted and vouchsafed to man to make actuality serve him to see the true by; language has coined the word 'poetry' to express this boom."

"Ah, so that is what you think," laughed Nanda. "According to that, and if one listens to you, poetry would also be the stupidity that comes after the cleverness, and, suppose a man is stupid, it is in order to ask whether he is still being stupid or being stupid again. I must say, you clever ones do not make it easy for the likes of us. We think the point is to become clever; but before one reaches it, one finds out the real point is to become stupid again. You ought not to show us the new and higher stages, for fear we lose courage to climb the first ones."

"From me," said Shridaman, "you have not heard that one must be clever. Come, let us stretch out in the soft grass after our meal and look through the branches of the trees into the sky. It is such a wonderful thing to look from a station which does not actually oblige us to look up, because the eyes are already directed upwards, and to see the sky in the way that Mother Earth sees it."

"Siya, be it so," Nanda agreed.

"Siyat!" Shridaman corrected him, in the pure tongue. Nanda laughed at himself and them both.

"Siyat, Siyat!" he repeated. "Hair-splitter, leave me my lingo! When I speak Sanskrit it sounds like the snuffling of a young heifer with a rope through her nose."

At this bucolic simile Shridaman too laughed

heartily; and they stretched themselves out as he had said and looked straight up through the swaying boughs and flowering bushes into the blue of Vishnu's heaven, waving broken-off branches to protect themselves from the red-and-white flies, called Children of Indra, that came to settle on their skins. Nanda had lain down, not because he cared in particular to look at the sky as Mother Earth did, merely out of good nature. He soon sat up again and resumed his Dravidian attitude, with a flower in his mouth.

"The Child of Indra is a confounded nuisance," he said, speaking of the darting host of flies as one and the same individual. "Probably he is attracted by my good mustard oil. Or it might be he has orders from his protector the elephant-rider, lord of the thunderbolt, the great god, to torment us as punishment—you know already why."

"That should not affect you," responded Shridaman; "for you voted under the tree that Indra's thanksgiving feast last autumn should be celebrated in the old or shall we rather say in the newer way, according to the ritual and the Brahmanic observance; you can wash your hands of the rest, even if we did afterwards in council decide otherwise and give Indra notice that we were turning to a newer or rather an older thanksgiving service, one which seems more natural to the religious feeling of us village folk than the patter the Brahmans reel off for Indra the Thunderer, who burst the strongholds of the aborigines."

"Certainly, as thy word sayeth, so is it," replied Nanda. "For my part, I still have an uncanny feeling, for even when I gave my voice under the tree for Indra, I was afraid he might not bother himself about such small matters and would just make all of us generally responsible for being done out of his feast at Welfare of Cows. Then it occurs to the people and comes into their heads, I don't know from where, that the Indra thanksgiving service is no longer the right thing, at least not for us shepherds and farmers, and we must think about pious simplification. What, said they, have we to do with the great Indra? The Brahmans, with their knowledge of the Vedas, may pay their homage with endless repetitions. As for us, we will sacrifice to the cows and mountains and forest meadows because they are our true and proper deities. And it seems to us that is what we had done before Indra came, who preceded the Coming One, and burst the strongholds of the aborigines; and even though we no longer rightly know what is to be done, yet it will come to us, and our hearts shall teach us. We will pay homage to our Bright Peak and his pastures, in our own countryside, with pious rites which are in so far new that we shall have to look for them in our hearts, remember and fetch them out again. To Bright Peak will we sacrifice the perfect of the herd, to him bring offerings of sour milk, flowers, fruit, and uncooked rice. Afterwards the herd of cows, wearing garlands of autumn flowers, shall rove over the mountain turning to him their right flanks, and the steers shall bellow to him with the thunder-voice of clouds heavy with rain. And that shall be our mountain worship, new and old. But in order that the Brahmans may have naught against it, we will feast them to the number of many hundreds; and from all the herds we will collect milk so that they can eat their fill of curds and rice-milk, and so may they be content. Thus spake some of those under the tree, and some agreed with them, but others did not. I voted from the first against the mountain rites, for I had great fear and reverence for Indra, who broke the strongholds of the blacks; and I do not hold with reviving things that nobody any longer rightly knows. But you spoke and uttered pure and right words—I mean right in respect to the language—in favour of the new form of the feast and for the renewal of the mountain rites over Indra's head, and so I was silent. For I thought: when those who have gone to school and learned something about the nature of being speak against Indra and in favour of simplification, then we others can have nothing to say, we can only hope that the great Comer and breaker of strongholds will have some judgement and be satisfied with the feeding of multitudes of Brahmans, so that he does not afflict us with drought or overwhelm us with rains. Perhaps, I thought, he is tired of his feast himself and thinks it would be more fun to have the mountain sacrifice and the procession of cows instead. We simple ones had great reverence for him; but perhaps he has not so much for himself these days. In the end I very much liked the revived rite and enjoyed helping to drive the garlanded cows about the mountain. Yet I will say, when you corrected my Prakrit and wanted me to say Siyat, it struck me again how strange it is that you are using your correct and cultured speech in the interest of sim-plification."

"You have no ground to reproach me," Shridaman answered, "for you yourself have been using the popular tongue to uphold the Brahman rites. You probably took pleasure in it. But let me tell you: there is far more pleasure in using correct and cultured words to support the claims of simplicity."

They were silent for a while. Shridaman still lay as he was and gazed up into the sky. Nanda held his stout arms clasped round his knees and looked between the trees down the slope towards the bathing-place of Mother Kali.

"Sh-h! Thunder and lightning! Bolts and blazes!" he whispered all of a sudden, and laid his finger to his thick lips. "Shridaman, brother, sit up and look very quietly. Going down to bathe, I mean. Open your eyes, it's worth the trouble! She cannot see us, but we can see her."

A young girl stood at the lonely shrine, about to perform the ritual of the bath. She had laid her sari and bodice on the steps and stood there quite nude, save only for some beads round her neck, her swaying ear-rings, and a white ribbon round her thick hair. The loveliness of her body was dazzling. Made of Maya it seemed, and of the most enchanting tint, neither too dark nor too pale, and more like a bronze with golden lights. Gloriously formed she was, after the thoughts of Brahma, with the sweetest childish shoulders, and hips deliciously curved, making a spacious pelvic cavity, with maidenly firm, budlike breasts and splendidly spreading buttocks that narrowed above to the smallest, most tender back. How supply it curved, as she raised her slender arms and clasped her hands at the back of her neck, so that the tender armpits showed darkly! In all this the most striking thing, the most

adequately representative of Brahma's thoughts—
yet without prejudice to the dazzling sweetness of
the breasts, which must infallibly win over any soul
to the life of sense—was the conjunction of this
magnificent rear with the slimness and pliant sup-
pleness of a back of elfin delicacy. By way of em-
phasis was the other contrast, between the splendid
swing of the hips—this of itself worthy of a whole
pæan of praise—and the dainty attenuation round
the waist. Just such a shape must have had the heavenly maid Pramlocha, sent by Indra to the ascetic
Kandu to wean him from his austerity lest he attain
to divine power.

"Let us withdraw," Shridaman said, as he sat
up, his eyes resting on the maiden's form. "It is not
right that she sees us not, yet we see her."

"Why not?" answered Nanda in a whisper.
"We were here first, to enjoy the peace and the
hush; and whatever else may come along, we cannot
help it. We will not stir; it would be cruel if we made
off, crackling the bushes, and she learned she had
been seen while she saw not. I look with pleasure—
you do not? Your eyes are red, as when you recite
text from the Rig-Veda."

"Be quiet!" Shridaman admonished him in
turn. "And be serious. This is a serious, a sacred
sight; that we look on at it is only excusable if we do
it with serious and pious minds."

"Yes, of course," answered Nanda. "Certainly
such a thing is no joke; but say what you like, it
is a pleasure. You wanted to look into the sky from
the flat earth. Now you see one can sometimes see
into heaven only by standing up and looking
straight ahead."

They were silent awhile, moved not at all, and looked. The gold-bronze maid did as they had done a little before, laid her cupped palms together and prayed, before descending to her purification. They saw her a little from one side, so it did not escape them that not only her body but her face as well, between the hanging ear-rings, was of the rarest sweetness: little nose, lips, brows, and especially the long slanting eyes like lotus leaves. She turned her head slightly, startling the friends lest she might be aware of them; and they could see that this charming figure suffered no least detraction from an ugly face; rather that harmony ruled throughout and the loveliness of the features fully bore out the loveliness of the form.

"But I know her!" Nanda suddenly murmured, with a snap of his fingers. "This very minute do I recognize her; only up to now did she escape me. That is Sita, daughter of Sumantra from the village of the Bisons near here. She came hither from her home to wash herself clean, of course. Why should I not know her? I swung her up to the sun."

"You swung her?" asked Shridaman, low-voiced but urgently. And Nanda replied:

"Why not? With all the strength of my arms, before all the people. In her clothes I should have known her at once. But who would recognize a naked person straight off? That's Sita of Bisonbull. I was there last spring to visit my aunt, and it was at the feast of aid to the sun; but she—"

"Later, I pray you," Shridaman interrupted in an anxious whisper. "The great good fortune that we may see her so close has also the misfortune that she might hear us. Not another word or we shall alarm her."

"Then she might run away and you would see her no more, and you have not seen your fill," Nanda said teasingly. But the other motioned him peremptorily, and once more they sat silent, watching Sita perform her ritual. She prayed first, then, with her face turned heavenwards, stepped cautiously into the pool, took up water and drank, and dipped in up to the crown of her head, on which she laid her hand. Afterwards for a while she dipped and played and slipped in and out; after a time she stepped back on dry land, cool and dripping and most beautiful to see. Even therewith was not quite an end to the favour vouchsafed to the friends; for after the purificatory bath the maid sat down on the steps that the sun might dry her. And her native charm, released by the conviction that she was quite alone, made her fall into first one, then another most pleasing posture. Only after some little time, and then only slowly, did she don her clothes and disappear up the temple stair.

"Well, that's all there is of that," said Nanda. "Now we can at least speak and move about. In the long run it gets tiresome to act as though you were not there."

"I do not see how you can use such a word," retorted Shridaman. "Could there be a more blissful state than to lose oneself in such a sight and be present only in its presence? I should have liked to hold my breath the whole time; not out of fear of losing sight of her face, but for fear of undeceiving her belief that she was alone; for that I trembled and felt myself sacredly responsible. She is called Sita, you say? I am glad to know, it consoles me for my offence, that I may pay her honour by name to myself. And you know her from swinging her?"

"As I tell you," Nanda assured him. "She was chosen as sun-maiden last spring when I was in her village, and I swung her in aid of the sun so high in the heavens that one could hardly hear her screams. Or else they were lost in the screaming of the crowd."

"You were lucky," said Shridaman. "You are always lucky. It must have been on account of your stout arms they chose you to swing her. I can just see how she rose and flew up into the blue. My imaginary picture of her flight blends with the one we saw just now, where she stood like a statue, bowed in prayer."

"Anyhow," said Nanda, "she has ground for prayer and penance; not on account of her behavior, for she is a very good girl, but on account of her looks. Certainly she cannot help them, yet after all, strictly speaking, she is responsible for them. A figure like that is taking. But why taking? Just because it takes us captive, makes us prisoners to the world of delights and desires. It tangles the beholder deeper in the snares of Samsara, so he simply loses consciousness just the way one loses one's breath. That is the effect she has even if it is not her intention. But her lengthening her eyes in the shape of a lotus leaf makes it look like intention. You may say the fine figure was given her, she did not deliberately take it, so she has nothing to repent on that score. But the truth is, there are cases where no real difference exists between 'given' and 'taken';

she knows that herself, probably she prays for pardon just because she is so 'taking.' This figure of hers, she has taken it—not as one just accepts something that is given, she really put it on, of herself. No amount of ritual bathing can alter that: she comes out with the very same taking behind she took in."

"You should not speak so coarsely," Shridaman chid him with feeling, "of such a tender and sacred being. True, you have ventured into the field of metaphysics, but I must tell you you express yourself very rustically there; and the use you make of what knowledge you have makes it clear you were not worthy of the vision. For everything depended on the spirit in which we looked on."

Nanda received the reproach in all modesty.

"Teach me, then, Dau-ji (elder brother)," he begged, "in what spirit you looked on and how I should have done."

"Lo," said Shridaman, "all beings have two sorts of existence: one for themselves and one for the eyes of others. They are, and also they are to be seen, soul and image; and ever is it sinful to let oneself be influenced by the image only and not to heed the soul. It is necessary to overcome the disgust inspired in us at sight of the scurvy beggar. We must not stop at the effect it has on our eyes and senses. For what affects us is impression, not reality; we must go behind it to reach the knowledge to which every phenomenon can lay claim, for it is more than phenomenon, and one must find the being, the soul, behind it. But not only shall we not stop at the disgust aroused in us by the sight of misery. Just as little must we dwell on the desire which the

image of the beautiful inspires; this too being more
than image, although the temptation of the senses
to take it only as such is perhaps even greater than
in the case of the repulsive beggar. The beautiful,
that is, seems to make no claim on our conscience,
no demand that we enter into its soul, whereas the
image of the beggar, by its very misery, does. Yet
we are equally guilty if we simply feast on the sight
of beauty without inquiring into its being. And our
debt to it is even greater, so it seems to me, if we
see it while it does not see us. Let me tell you, Nanda, it was a real boon to me that you could name
the name of her whom we watched, Sita, daughter
of Sumantra; for it gave me to know something of
that which is more than the image, since the name
is a part of the essence and of the soul. Happier still
I was to hear from you that she is a good maiden;
for that was a means still more easily to go behind
her image and understand her soul. And then her
lengthening her eyes in the shape of a lotus leaf, and
painting the lashes a little—that, you might say, is
all only custom and has nothing to do with morality;
she does it in all innocence, her morals being de-
pendent upon convention. But, after all, beauty too
has a duty towards its image; perhaps in fulfilling it
she only seeks to increase the desire to ask after her
soul. I like to imagine that she has a good father in
Sumantra, and a careful mother, and has been
brought up in piety; I can fancy her life and occupa-
tions as daughter of the house, how she grinds the
corn on the stone, makes the porridge on the hearth,
or spins the wool to a fine thread. Having been
guilty of beholding her image, my heart cries out
to have it become a person."

"That I can understand," responded Nanda. "But you must remember that this wish cannot be so lively with me, since she already was more of a person to me, because I swung her up to the sun."

"Only too much," replied Shridaman, whose voice had betrayed a certain quiver throughout. "Obviously only too much; for this familiarity which you were vouchsafed—whether with justice or not, I will not say, for you owed it to your stout arms and your whole sturdy body, not to your head and the thoughts of your head—this familiarity seems to have made her entirely a material being in your eyes and dulled your gaze for the higher meaning of such a phenomenon. Otherwise you would not have spoken with such unpardonable coarseness of the fine shape it has taken on. Do you not know, then, that in every female shape—child, maid, mother, or grey-haired woman—*she*, the All-Mother, hides herself, the all-nourisher, Sakti, the great goddess; of whose womb all things come, into whose womb all things go; whom we honour and praise in every manifestation that bears her sign? In her most worshipful shape she has revealed herself to us here on the bank of the little stream Gold-fly; shall we not then be most deeply moved by her revealing herself thus—to the extent that in fact, now that I notice it, my voice somewhat trembles— though that may in part be due to displeasure at your manner of speaking?"

"And your cheeks and forehead are red as fire," said Nanda, "and your voice, though it trembles, has a fuller ring than common. I can assure you that I too in my way was quite affected."

"Then I do not understand," answered Shri-

daman, "how you can talk so inadequately and reproach her for her fine figure that so confuses people that the breath of consciousness goes out
of them! That is to look at things with culpable
one-sidedness and to show yourself entirely empty
of the true and real essence of her who revealed herself to us in so sweet an image. For she is All and not
only one; life and death, madness and wisdom, en-
chantress and liberatress, knowest thou not that?
Knowest only that she befools and bewitches the
host of created beings and not also that she leads
them out beyond the darkness of confusion to
knowledge of the truth? Then you know very little
and have not grasped a great and difficult mystery:
that the very drunkenness she puts upon us is the
same as the exaltation which bears us on to truth
and freedom. For so it is, that what enchains us frees
us, and that exaltation it is that binds together beauty
of sense and beauty of spirit."

Nanda's black eyes glittered with tears, for he
was easily moved and could scarcely listen to metaphysical language without weeping; especially at
this moment, when Shridaman's otherwise rather
thin voice had suddenly taken on a deep note that
went to his heart. He drew a breath like a sob
through his goat-nose as he said:

"How you speak today, Dau-ji, so solemnly!
I think I have never heard you speak so strangely;
it touches me very near. I could wish you would not
go on, I feel it so much. And yet I beg you to, do
please go on about the spirit and the chains and the
All-Embracing one!"

"So you see," Shridaman went on in his exalted
strain, "the meaning of it all, and how it is not only

madness but wisdom that she confers. If what I say
moves you, it is because she is mistress of the fluent
word, mingled with the wisdom of Brahma. In
her twofold shape we recognize her greatness; for
she is the wrathful one, black and terrifying, drink-
ing the blood of creatures out of steaming vessels;
but at the same time is she the white and gracious
one, source of all being, cherishing all forms of life
at her nourishing breast. Vishnu's great Maya is she,
she holds him embraced, he dreams in her; but we
dream in him. Many waters flow into the eternal
Ganges, but the Ganges flows into the sea. So we
flow into Vishnu's world-dreaming godhead; but
that into the sea of the Mother. Lo, we came
to a place where our life-dream flowed into the
sacred bathing-place, and there appeared to us the
All-Mother, the All-Consumer, in whose womb
we bathed, in her sweetest shape, to amaze and to
exalt us—very likely as a reward, because we honoured her procreative emblem and poured water
to it. Linga and Yoni—there is no greater sign and
no greater hour in life than when the man is sum-
moned with his Sakti to circle round the bridal fire,
their hands are united with the flowery bond and he
speaks the words: 'I have received her!' When he
takes her from the hand of her parents and speaks
the royal word: 'He am I, this is you; heaven I, earth
you; I the music of the song, you the words; so shall
we make the journey together.' When they cele-
brate the meeting—no longer human beings more,
not he and she, one male, one female, but the great
pair, he Siva, she Durga, the high and awful goddess; when their words wander and are no more
their words, but a stammering out of the drunken

deeps and they die away to the highest life in the supernal joy of their embrace. Such is the holy hour which laves us in wisdom and grants us release from the delusions of the ego in the womb of the Mother. For as sense and spirit flow together in rapture, so do life and death in love!"

Nanda was utterly ravished by these metaphysical words.

"My goodness," said he, shaking his head, while the tears sprang from his eyes, "but the goddess Speech is gracious to you, endowing you with the wisdom of Brahma till I can hardly bear to listen, yet would have you go on for ever. If I could sing and say even a fifth part of all that comes out of your headpiece I would love and honour myself in all my members. That is why you are so necessary to me, my elder brother; what I have not you have, and you are my friend, so that it is almost as though I had it myself. For as your fellow I have a part in you, and so I am a little bit Shridaman; but without you I were only Nanda, and that is not enough. I tell you freely, I could not bear to survive a parting from you; I would erect the funeral pyre and burn myself. So much for that. Take this before we go!"

And he rummaged in his bundle with his dark beringed hands and drew out a roll of betel, such as is pleasant to chew after the meal to give sweet odour to the mouth. This he handed to Shridaman, with his face averted and wet with tears, as a present-giving and a sign and seal to their friendship and their compact.

4

So they went on, and their respective errands took them for a time upon different ways. When they had reached the river Jumna with its crowding sails and saw on the horizon the outline of the city Kurukshetra, Shridaman took to the highroad full of ox-carts and entered the narrow city streets to seek the house of the man from whom he was to buy the rice-mallets and firewood. Nanda struck off on a narrow lane leading to the mud huts of the lowly folk who were to give him crude iron for his father's smithy. They blessed each other and took their leave, agreeing to meet again on this same spot at a certain hour on the third day, their business being done, and then to return home as they had come.

But when the sun had risen three times, Nanda, riding a grey ass which he had got from the lowly folk to transport his iron, had to wait some time at the place of parting and meeting, for Shridaman was late. At length he came along the highway with his pack; his steps were slow and dragging, his cheeks hollow in the soft fan-shaped beard, and his eyes full of gloom. He showed no joy at sight of his friend, and when Nanda hastened to take his burden and put it on the ass, Shridaman's manner did not change; he walked by Nanda's side, as drooped and depressed as before, his words were hardly more than Yea, yea, even when they ought to have been Nay, nay. He did say no, too, but precisely when he should have said yes, namely at the hour for rest and refreshment, when he declared he would not and could not eat. In answer to a question, he also said that he could not sleep.

All this looked like illness. Indeed, when on the second evening they were walking along by the light of the stars, and the anxious Nanda got him to speak a few words, he not only said that he was ill, but also added in a strangled voice that the illness was incurable, a sickness unto death. It was of such a nature, he said, that he not only must but would die, the must and the will being entirely interwoven and indistinguishable, so that they formed a single compelling desire, each issuing inevitably from the other. "If you are serious in your friendship," he said to Nanda, always in that strangled, wildly agitated voice, "then do me love's last service and build me the funeral hut that I may go into it and burn in the fire. For the incurable disease burns me within with such torments that the consuming ardour of the fire will feel by contrast like soothing oil and a healing bath in the holy stream."

Oh, ye great gods, what will become of you? thought Nanda when his ears heard this. But we must say that despite his goat-nose and his physical habit, which stood midway between the lowly folk who had sold him his iron and Shridaman the grandchild of Brahmans, Nanda was equal to the difficult situation and did not lose his head in face of his companion's morbid state, however high-class. He made use of the advantage which the sound person has over the ailing, and, suppressing his inclination to shudder, loyally put himself at his friend's service and spoke with reason and tact.

"You may be sure," said he, "if it is true, as you say, and as I cannot doubt, that your ailment is incurable, I will not hesitate to carry out your directions and erect the pyre for you. And I will make it large enough that after I have kindled it there will be room for me beside you; for I do not think to survive the parting an hour, but will enter with you into the flames. Just for that reason, and because the thing concerns me too so nearly, you must tell me what is the matter and call your illness by name, if only so that I may gain the conviction of its incurableness and prepare to turn us both into ashes. You must admit that what I say is right and just, and if even I with my limited understanding see that, how much more must you, the wiser, agree! If I put myself in your place and try to use your head as though it sat on my shoulders, I cannot but think that my —I mean your—conviction of the incurableness of your disease needs confirmation and proof by others before we begin to carry out such far-reaching intentions. And therefore speak!"

For a long time the lank-cheeked Shridaman would not come out with it; he declared that the mortal hopelessness of his sufferings needed no evidence and no explanation. But at last after much urging he complied, with the following confession, putting as he spoke one hand over his eyes, that he need not look at his friend.

"Since," said he, "we watched that maiden, nude but virtuous, whom you once swung up to the sun, Sita, daughter of Sumantra, at the bathing-place of Devi, suffering to do with her nakedness as well as her virtue, and having its origin in both, has been planted like a seed in my soul and there flourished until it has penetrated all my limbs down to their smallest fibre; consumed my mental powers, robbed me of sleep and appetite, and now slowly but surely leads me on to destruction." He went on to say that his anguish was mortal because the cure —namely, the fulfilment of the wishes founded in the beauty and virtue of the maiden—was unthinkable, unimaginable, and of an extravagance, in short, far beyond mortal pretensions. If a man were afflicted by desire for a happiness of which no mortal but only a god might dream, and if he could not live without this happiness, then it was clear the man must die. "If," he concluded, "I may not possess her, Sita of the partridge-eyes, the glorious colour, the divine hips, then of itself my spirit will dissolve and pass away. So build me the pyre, for only in the fire is salvation from the conflict of the human and the divine. It pains me that you would enter it with me, on account of your youth and your blithe young nature and lucky-calf lock; yet there is some justice in it too. For the thought that you swung her up to the sun adds to the fire in my breast, and I should hate to leave upon earth anyone to whom this had been granted."

Nanda had no sooner heard Shridaman out than to his friend's utter amazement he burst out laughing, and continued to laugh as he danced up and down and embraced his friend by turns.

"Lovesick!" he cried. "Lovesick, lovesick! That is all there is to it. That is the mortal illness. What fun, what a joke!" And he began to sing:

"The clever man, the clever man,
How wisely did he reason!

But now, alack, his wits are gone,
His wisdom's out of season.

The glances of a maiden's eye
Have turned his head to jelly;
A monkey tumbled from a tree
Could not look half so silly!"

Then he went on roaring, clapping his hands on his knees, and crying out:

"Shridaman, brother, how I rejoice to know it is nothing worse, and you are only thinking of the funeral pyre because your heart is on fire like a straw thatch! The little witch stood there too long in your sight; Kama, the god with the flowery arrow, has pierced you through. What we thought was the humming of bees was the whirr of his bolt; and Rati, sister of the springtime and desire, she has done this to you. And it is all quite normal and jolly, happens every day, and is no more than proper to a man. To you it looks as though only a god could hope for such bliss; but that only shows the warmth of your desires, and proves that they do indeed come from a god, that is to say Kama, but not that they are fitting to him instead of to you. Take it not unfriendly, but only as cooling counsel to your overheated sense, when I say that you are mistaken if you think only gods have a right to the goal of your desires. That is exaggerated; indeed, nothing is more human and natural than that you are driven to sow in this furrow." (He put it like this because the word Sita means a furrow.) "But to you," he went on, "the proverb applies: 'The owl is blind by day, by night the crow. But whom love blinds nor light nor darkness know.' I repeat this edifying saying that you may see yourself in it and bethink you that Sita of Bisonbull is no goddess, although she might so seem to you as she stood naked at the bathing-place of Durga, but a quite ordinary though extremely pretty little thing; she lives like other people, grinds the corn, cooks the porridge, and spins the wool and has parents who are like other folk, even though Sumantra, her father, can boast of a little warrior blood in his veins—too far away to amount to much! In short, they are people one can talk to; and why have you a friend like your Nanda if he should not get on his legs and fix up this whole quite regular and ordinary business for you, so you can be happy? Well? Hey? What, stupid! Instead of laying the bonfire and squatting in it beside you, I will help you build your bridal house where you can live in bliss with your bride of the beautiful hips!"

Shridaman, after a pause, answered and said: "Your words—not to mention your song—contained much that was offensive. For offensive it is to call my anguished desires quite ordinary and everyday when they are past my power to endure and are nigh to split my heart in twain. A yearning stronger than we are, too strong to sustain—we are right in calling it unfitting for man, only fit for a god to know. But I am sure you mean well by me, you want to console me, so I forgive you the vulgar and ignorant way you express yourself about my mortal illness. Indeed, not only do I forgive you; for your last words seem to hold out a possibility which has already stimulated my heart, but now resigned to death, to new and violent throbbing. It is the picture you hold up that has done this, though as yet I am

incapable of belief in it. I have moments of divin-
ing that unscathed mortals, in another frame of mind
than mine, may be able to judge more clearly and
objectively. But I immediately mistrust any other
view than my own and believe only in the way
which points me to death. Consider how probable
it is that the divine Sita was contracted in marriage
as a child and is soon to be united with a bride-
groom who grew up with her! The mere thought
is such a burning torment that I can only flee from
it into the coolness of the funeral pyre."

But Nanda swore by their friendship that his
fear was utterly baseless; Sita was not bound by any
child-marriage. Her father Sumantra had objected
to such an arrangement, on the ground that it
would expose her to the ignominy of widowhood in
case the boy husband died untimely. In fact, she
could not have been chosen as the swinging maiden
if she had been betrothed. No, Sita was free, she was
in the market; and with Shridaman's good caste, his
family connections and his conversance with the
Vedas, it only needed that he formally commission
his friend to take the thing in hand and set in motion the negotiations between the families, to make
a happy issue to the affair as good as certain.

Shridaman's cheek had twitched with pain at
mention of the swinging episode. But on the whole
he showed himself grateful for his friend's readi-
ness to serve him. Slowly he let himself be turned
by Nanda's sound reasoning away from his yearning for death towards a belief that the fulfilment
of his desire, to enfold Sita as a bride in his arms,
did not lie outside the realms of the possible and human. Even so, he stuck to it that if the wooing went

wrong, Nanda would have to erect the funeral pyre
with his stout arms. The son of Garga soothed him
by promising this; but found it more pertinent to
discuss in detail all the steps leading up to the happy
consummation. Shridaman was to retire entirely
and await the issue; Nanda for his part had first to
open the affair to Bhavabhuti, Shridaman's father,
and persuade him to undertake negotiations with
the maiden's parents. Then Nanda, representing
the wooer, would betake himself as suitor of the
bride to Bisonbull and in his character of friend
carry out the further approach between the couple.

No sooner said than done. Bhavabhuti, the
vanija of Brahman stock, was rejoiced at the com-
munication which his son's friend made to him.
Sumantra, the cow-breeder, of warrior blood, was
not displeased by the proposals, accompanied by
considerable presents. Nanda in homely but con-
vincing words sang the praises of his friend in the
house of the wooing. Not less auspicious was the return visit of Sita's parents to Welfare of Cows, to
convince themselves of the suitor's good faith. In
such exchanges as these the days passed, and the
maiden Sita learned from afar to see in Shridaman, the merchant's son, her destined lord and
master. The marriage contract was drawn up and
the signing of it celebrated with a feast and the exchange of appropriate gifts. The day of the wedding, selected by advice of those learned in the heavenly signs, drew on; and Nanda, who knew that it
would do so—quite aside from the fact that Shridaman's union with Sita was fixed for it, which pre-
vented Shridaman from believing it would ever
come—ran about inviting kin and friends to the

nuptials. The nuptial bonfire was laid on a base of cakes of dried dung in the inner court of Sita's parents' house. Nanda's strong arms did yeoman service here too; while the priest of Brahma stood by and recited texts.

So came on the day when Sita the fine-limbed, her body anointed with sandalwood, camphor, and coconut oils, adorned with jewellery, in wedding bodice and robe, her head enveloped in a cloudy veil, for the first time set eyes on her appointed husband. He, as we are aware, had seen her before. For the first time she called him by his name. The hour had indeed been waited for, but here it was at last and took on presentness, when he spoke the words: "I have received her"; when with offerings of rice and butter he took her from her parents' hands, called himself heaven and her earth, himself the melody, her the words; and to the singing and hand-clapping of the women went with her thrice round the glowing fire. Then in solemn procession, with a team of white bulls he led her home to his village and to his mother's heart.

Here there were more good-luck ceremonies to be performed, here too they went round about the fire; he fed her with sugar-cane, let the ring fall in her lap. At the festal meal they sat again with kin and friends. But when they had eaten and drunk and been sprinkled with rose-water and water from the Ganges, they were accompanied by all the guests to the bridal chamber or "room of the happy pair," where the flower-garlanded bed had been set up. There, among kisses, jesting, and tears, everyone took leave of them. Nanda, who had been at their side throughout, was last upon the threshold.

5

Here we warn the listener, perhaps misled by the so far pleasing course of the tale, not to fall prey to a misconception of its real character. For a little space there was silence, it turned its face away; when it turns back it is no more the same, but changed to a frightful mask, a face of horror, distracting, Medusalike, turning the beholder to stone, or maddening him to wild acts of abnegation—for so Shridaman, Nanda, and Sita saw it, on the journey which they—but everything in its turn.

Six months had passed since Shridaman's mother had taken the lovely Sita upon her lap and Sita had granted to her narrow-nosed husband the full enjoyment of wedded bliss. The heavy summer had passed, and now the rainy season, covering the sky with floods of cloud, the earth with freshets of flowers, would soon be over too. Heaven's tent was spotless, the autumn lotus was in bloom, when the newly wedded pair discussed with their friend Nanda, after winning the consent of Shridaman's parents, a visit to Sita's family. Her parents had not seen her since she embraced her husband, and they wished to convince themselves that her wedded bliss became her. Although Sita had begun of late to look forward to the joys of motherhood, they ventured on the journey, which was not long and in the cool of the year not very trying.

They travelled in a car with a top and side curtains, drawn by a zebu and a dromedary; friend Nanda being the driver. He sat in front of the wedded pair, his little cap on one ear and his legs dangling down. He seemed to be paying too much attention to his driving to turn round often to speak to his passengers. Sometimes he called out to his beasts; from time to time he burst into song, very loud and clear—but after the first notes his voice would die down to a humming, ending in a vague chirrup to his team. If the burst of song was rather startling, like a relief to an overcharged breast, its dying away was no less so.

Behind him the wedded pair sat silent. They had Nanda immediately before them, their gaze if directed straight ahead would rest on the back of his neck; as the young wife's sometimes did, rising slowly from contemplation of her lap and after a short pause swiftly returning there. Shridaman avoided the sight entirely, keeping his face averted towards the canvas curtains. Gladly would he have changed places with Nanda and become the driver, in order not to have, like his wife beside him, a view of the brown back with the spinal column and the flexible shoulder-blades. But it was no matter, he thought; for any other arrangement would have been no better. And so in silence they took their way, but the breath of all three came quickly as though they had been running; their eyes were blood-shot, and that is always a bad sign. A person gifted with second sight would certainly have seen a shadow, like a black pinion, covering them as they drove.

And they drove, by preference, in the shadow of darkness; in other words, before the dawn; thus avoiding the burden of the midday sun—a sensible course, for which, however, they had other grounds than good sense. The confusion of their own souls was favoured by the darkness, and unconsciously they projected their inward bewilderment into outward space—with the result that they lost their way. Nanda did not guide his zebu and dromedary into the turning off the highroad that led to Sita's home. With no moon, and only the stars to guide him, he took the wrong turn, and the road they found themselves on was soon no road at all, but only a thinning among the trees, and even that only apparent, for they thickened again and became a forest wherein the thinning soon disappeared through which they might have made their way back.

It was impossible to get forwards with their cart among the tree-trunks and on the soft floor of the forest. They confessed to each other that they had gone astray; but not that they had brought about a situation corresponding to the confusion of their own minds. Shridaman and Sita, sitting behind Nanda as he drove, had not even been asleep; open-eyed, they allowed him to take them into the wrong road. There was nothing for it but to make a fire where they were, and await the sunrise with more security against beasts of prey. When day at length dawned, they cast about in all directions; unharnessed their team and let them go single file; then with great difficulty pushed and shoved the cart wherever the teak and sandalwood trees would let them through, and reached the edge of the jungle, where they found a stone gulley. This might be possible for the cart; and Nanda declared that it would certainly lead in the direction of Sita's home.

Following the steep gulley, with many jolts, they came on a temple hewed out of the rock, and recognized it as a shrine of Devi, Durga the terrible and unapproachable, Kali the dark Mother. Obeying an impulse of his heart, Shridaman expressed a wish to get out and pay honour to the goddess. "I will only look at her, say a prayer, and come back in a few minutes," he said to his companions. "Just wait here!" And he left the waggon and clambered up the rude steps leading to the temple.

It was a shrine no more important than the little mother-house by the secluded bathing-place on the river Goldfly; but its columns and ornamentation had been carved with infinite piety and care. The entrance seemed to crouch beneath the wild mountain itself, supported by columns flanked by snarling leopards. There were painted pictures to right and left, also at the sides of the inner entrance, carven out of the rock; visions of life in the flesh, all jumbled together, just as life is, out of skin and bones, marrow and sinews, sperm and sweat and tears and ropy rheum, filth and urine and gall; thick with passions, anger, lust, envy, and despair; lovers' partings and bonds unloved; with hunger, thirst, old age, sorrow, and death; all this for ever fed by the sweet, hot streaming blood-stream, suffering and enjoying in a thousand shapes, teeming, devouring, turning into one another. And in that all-encompassing labyrinthine flux of the animal, human, and divine, there would be an elephant's trunk that ended in a man's hand, or a boar's head seemed to take the place of a woman's. —Shridaman heeded not the pictures, he thought not to see them; yet his red-veined eyeballs skimmed them in passing,

and they stirred in his soul feelings of slight giddiness and tender pity, to prepare it for the beholding of the Mother.

Twilight reigned in the rocky cell, lighted only
from above by rays falling through the mountain
into the audience hall, which he crossed to go into
the lower vestibule adjoining it. There a door on a
still lower level, to which steps led down, admitted
him into the heart of the house, the womb of the
great Mother.

At the foot of the steps he trembled and staggered back, his hands spread out against the two
linga stones on either side. Kali's image was fear-
some. Did it only seem so to his blood-shot eyes, or
had he never anywhere beheld the raging one in
such triumphantly horrible guise? Framed in an
arch composed of skulls and hacked-off hands and
feet, the idol stood out from the living rocky wall
in colours that snatched up all the light to hurl it
glaringly back. She was adorned with a dazzling
crown; clothed and girt with bones and severed
limbs, and her eighteen arms were a whirling wheel.
Swords and fiery beacons the Mother brandished.
Blood steamed hot in the skull she held with one
hand to her lips, and blood was at her feet in a
spreading pool. The frightful one stood in a bark on
the flooding sea of life, it swam in a sea of blood.
The very smell of blood saluted Shridaman's thin
nostrils, it smelt old and sweetish in the stagnant air
of this mountain cave, this subterranean charnel-
house, where coagulating blood choked and made
sticky the runnels in the pavement grooved to carry
off the quick-flowing life-stream of the beheaded
sacrifices. Four or five heads of animals, bison, swine,

and goats, their eyes open and glazed, were piled in a pyramid on the altar before the image of the Unescapable, and the sword that had served to behead them, sharp-edged and shining, though spotted with dried blood, lay on the flags at one side.

Shridaman stared at the wild glaring visage, his horror mounting by the moment to fever heat. This was She, the Deathbringer-Lifegiver, Compeller of sacrifice—her whirling arms made his own senses go round in drunken circles. He pressed his clenched fists against his mightily throbbing breast; uncanny shudderings, cold and hot, surged over his frame in successive floods. In the back of his head, in the very pit of his stomach, in the woeful excitation of his organs of sex, he felt one single urge, driving on to the extremity of a deed against his own life in the service of the eternal womb. With lips already bloodless he prayed:

"Beginningless, that wast before all created! Mother without man, whose garment none lifteth! All-embracing horror and desire, sucking back into thyself the worlds and images thou givest forth! With offerings of living creatures the people honour thee, for to thee is due the life-blood of all! How shall I not find grace to my healing, if I bring thee myself as offering? Well I know I shall not thereby escape life, even though that were desirable. But let me enter again into thee through the door of the womb that I may be free of this self; let me no more be Shridaman, to whom all desire is but bewilderment, since it is not he who gives it!"

Spoke these darkling words, seized up the sword from the floor, and severed his own head from his neck.

Quickly said; and not otherwise than quickly done. Yet the teller has here but one wish: that the hearer may not accept the fact with thoughtless indifference, as something quite common and natural, simply because it has been often told and stands in the records, that people practise cutting off their own heads. The single case is never common—the most common of all the things we think and talk about are birth and death; yet attend at a birth or a deathbed and ask yourself, ask the groaning or the parting soul, whether it is common or not. Self-beheading, however often it may be reported, is an act well-nigh impossible; to carry it through takes enormous determination, a fearful summoning up of purpose and energy. That Shridaman, the little Brahman with the mild pensive eyes and thin clerkly arms, did in fact perpetrate it, must not be taken as in the common run, but as something scarcely credible at all.

Enough, in all conscience, that he performed the gruesome sacrifice in the twinkling of an eye; here lay his noble head, with the soft beard on the cheeks, and there his body, that less important appendage, its two hands still grasping the sacrificial sword by the hilt. From the trunk the blood gushed out and ran into the channels in the floor. There was only a slight incline; so once in the channels it crept but slowly towards the pit under the altar —very like the little river Goldfly, that comes rushing, like a colt let loose, out of Himawant's gate but flows more and more quietly as it nears its mouth.

❀ *6* ❀

Returning now from the bowels of this rocky cell back to the pair waiting outside, we need not be surprised that they spent the first part of the time in silence, but after that began to question aloud. After all Shridaman had only wanted to make a brief devotion; where was he lingering so long? The lovely Sita, sitting behind Nanda in the cart, had gazed by turns at his neck and into her lap and kept as still as he, whose goat-nose and thick lips remained turned towards his team. But at length both began to wriggle in their seats, and after a while friend Nanda resolutely turned round to the young wife and asked:

"Have you any idea why he keeps us waiting and what he is doing there so long?"

"I cannot imagine, Nanda," responded she, in the sweet lilting and trilling voice he had been afraid to hear. She had quite superfluously added his name, and he had been afraid of that too—it was unnecessary, and he himself had not said: "Where is Shridaman," but simply: "Where is he?"

"I have been wondering a long time," she went on, "and if you had not turned round to me and asked me, I should very soon have asked you."

He shook his head, partly out of surprise at his friend's delay, but partly to ward off the unnecessary words she always used. "Turned round" would have been enough, the "to me," although quite correct, was unnecessary and even dangerous, spoken as it was while they waited for Shridaman, and in that sweetly lilting, slightly affected voice.

He said nothing, afraid lest he too might speak in an unnatural voice and address her by her name, for he felt drawn to follow the example she had set. It was she who after a short pause made the suggestion:

"I will tell you what, Nanda, you must go after him and see where he is, give him a shake with those strong arms of yours, if he has forgotten himself in prayer—we cannot wait any longer, and it is very strange of him to leave us sitting here, and waste the time while the sun is getting higher. We are late anyhow by reason of losing the way, and my parents must be beginning to worry about me, for they love me beyond aught in the world. Do pray go fetch him, Nanda! Even though he does not want to come and protests a little, yet make him come. You are stronger than he."

"Good, I will go fetch him," Nanda replied. "Of course in all friendliness. I need only remind him of the time. It was my fault we lost the way. I had already thought of going, and only feared you might not like to wait here alone. But it is only for a few seconds."

With that he lowered himself from the driver's seat and went up into the shrine.

And we, who know what a sight awaited him there! We must accompany him through the audience hall where he walked all unconscious; and through the vestibule where still he was unaware; then finally down into the mother-cell. Now, indeed, he faltered, he staggered, a dull cry of horror on his lips, struggling to hold fast to the linga stones, just as Shridaman had done. But his horror was not, like Shridaman's, for the image, but for the awful sight on the floor. There lay his friend, the waxen face with loosened neckcloth severed from the trunk, his blood flowing by many ways towards the pit.

Poor Nanda quivered like an elephant's ear. He held his cheeks with his dark beringed hands and from between his thick lips came chokingly over and over the name of his friend. He bent and made helpless motions towards the two parts of him on the ground, not knowing which part to embrace or to address. To the head he turned at last, that having always been so decidedly the main part; knelt down to the pallid shape and spoke, his goat-nosed face awry with bitter weeping. He laid one hand on the body and turned to it now and again as he talked.

"Shridaman," he sobbed, "dear friend, what hast thou done, and how couldst thou bring thy-self to do this with thy hands and arms, a deed so hard to do! It was not anything for thee! No one urged thee to this, yet hast thou accomplished it. Always have I admired thy spirit, now must I in tears admire thy body too, because thou hast been able to do this hardest of all deeds! But what must have gone on in thy soul, to bring thee to it! How in thy breast must generosity and despair have gone hand in hand, in sacrificial dance, ere thou couldst slay thyself! Oh woe, Oh, woe! Severed the fine head from the fine body! Still remains the soft fat-ness where it was, but reft of sense and meaning, unallied with that noble head of thine. Say, am I guilty? Am I indeed guilty of thy death by my very being, if also not by my act? Lo, since my head still thinks, I try to think as thou wouldst, and perhaps in thy wisdom thou wouldst have called the guilt of being more essential than that of action. But what more can a man do than avoid acting? I have kept silent as much as possible in order not to speak with a cooing voice. I have said no unnecessary word, nor added her name when I addressed her. I am my own witness, there is indeed no other, that I took no advantage when she carped at you. But what good is all that, when I am guilty by my very existence in the flesh? I should have gone into the desert and as an anchorite performed strict observance! I ought to have done it, without any word from you, I confess it humbly. But in my defence I can say that had you spoken I would have done it! Why did you never speak, dear head, before you lay there sundered and still sat on your shoulders? Always have our heads spoken together, yours wise and mine simple; yet in the most serious and dangerous concern of all, then you were silent! Now it is too late; you have not spoken, you have acted greatly and cruelly and shown me how I too must act. Surely you did not believe I would fail you, that my stout arms would falter at a deed your slender ones have carried out! Often have I told you I did not think to survive a parting from you; when in your lovesickness you ordered me to build the funeral hut, I declared to you that if I did it at all I would do it for two and squat inside it with you. What now must happen I long have known, even though only now does it stand out clear from the confusion of my thoughts when I came in and saw you lying—by 'you' I mean body there and head here beside it—then was Nanda's resolve made on the instant. I would have burned with you, so will I also bleed with you, for nothing else remains to me. Shall I go out to her to tell her what you have done, and in the cries of horror she will utter hear her secret joy? Shall I go about with tarnished name and have people say, as they certainly will: 'The villain Nanda has wronged his friend, has murdered him out of lust for his wife?' No, not that! Not ever that. I will follow you, and may the eternal womb drink my blood with yours!"

Thus saying, he turned from the head to the body, loosed the hilt of the sword from the already stiffening fingers, and with his stout arms carried out most thoroughly the sentence he himself had pronounced; so that his body, to mention it first, fell across Shridaman's, and his simple head bounced alongside that of his friend, where it lay with its eyes rolled up. But his blood too burst quick and furiously forth and then trickled slowly through the runnels to the mouth of the pit.

7

Meanwhile, Sita, the furrow, sat outside, alone in her tented cart, and the time was longer to her because she had no nape of a neck to look at any more. What—while she yielded to quite common-place feelings of impatience—was happening to that neck, of course she refused to dream. —Possibly, in her inmost soul—far beneath her ill-humour, which was lively, but belonged to the sphere of small possible mischances, and merely made her scuffle with her feet—the suspicion stirred of something frightful, some explanation of the delay which would make impatience and annoyance irrelevant because it belonged to an order of possibilities beyond the scope of kicking and scuffling. We must reckon with a secret receptivity of the young wife for imaginings of this order, because she had been living under certain conditions, and having certain experiences, which, to put it mildly, were themselves rather extravagant in their nature. But nothing of that sort entered into the things she was saying to herself.

"It is just unspeakable, it is almost unbearable," she thought. "Men are all alike, one must not set one above another, for there is no dependence on any. One of them leaves you sitting with the other, so that he deserves I don't know what for it; and when you send the other, then you sit here alone. And that with the sun getting high, because we had already lost so much time. I shall soon fly out of my skin with rage. There is not a single excuse, in the whole range of reasonable, sensible possibilities, for one disappearing and then the other too. The utmost I can think is that they have fallen foul of each other, because Shridaman is so set on praying that he will not stir from the spot, and Nanda is trying to force him, but out of respect for my husband's weak frame will not use his full strength; for if he wanted to, he could carry him like a child in his arms; they feel like iron when one happens to touch them. It would be humiliating for Shridaman, yet the annoyance almost makes me wish Nanda would do just that. I must say, you both deserve I should take the reins and drive on alone to my parents, and you would find me gone when you finally came out. If it were not so embarrassing to arrive alone like that, without husband or friend, because both of them went and left me, I would just do it straight off. Otherwise all I can do—and it is certainly high time—is to go after them and see what in the world they are up to. No wonder I feel somewhat alarmed, being with child as I am, at their strange behavior, for fear of what is behind it. But the worst thing I can think of, after all, is that for some reason unknown, they have quarrelled, and the quarrel is keeping them from coming back. I will just step in and straighten them both out."

With that the lovely Sita got down from the cart, her hoops billowing beneath her enveloping garment, and betook herself to the shrine—and fifteen seconds later she was confronted by that most hideous of sights.

She flung up her arms, her eyes started from their sockets; bereft of her senses she sank full length

on the ground. But that helped her not at all, the
situation would keep, it had been keeping all the
time Sita waited; and it would keep on keeping.
When the unhappy Sita came to herself it was still
there. She tried to faint again, but thanks to her
sound constitution she could not. So she cowered
on the stone pavement, her fingers in her hair, and
stared at the severed heads, the bodies lying across
each other, and all the crawling blood.

"Ye gods, saints, and holy hermits!" she whispered blue-lipped, "I am lost! Both men, both at
once. All is over! My lord and husband, who went
about the fire with me, my Shridaman with the es-
timable head and the body, which after all was warm
for he taught me lust, as far as I know it, in nights
of holy wedlock—severed the honoured head from
the body, lost and gone. Lost and gone—and the
other, Nanda, who swung me and wooed me for
Shridaman—severed and bleeding body from head
—there he lies, the lucky-calf lock still on his breast
—once so merry, but headless, what now? I could
touch him, I could feel the strength and beauty of
his arms and thighs, if I would. But I care not, blood
and death have set a barrier between him and wan-
ton desire as honour and friendship did before. They
have cut off each other's heads! For a reason I no
longer conceal from myself, their anger blazed up,
like a fire on which one has thrown butter; their
strife was such that it came to this mutual deed—I
see all clearly. But only one sword is here—and
Nanda holds it! How could they fight with only
one? Shridaman, forgotten all wisdom and mild-
ness, seized the sword and hewed off Nanda's head,
who then—but no! It was Nanda, for reasons at

which I shudder, beheaded Shridaman, who then—
oh no, oh no! Think of it no more, it avails nothing,
there is nothing but blood and darkness in the darkness of this horrible place, and only one thing is
clear, they behaved like savages and not for a moment thought of me. Or rather, of course they
thought of me, their horrible masculine deed was
on my account, poor thing, I shudder at the
thought. But only with reference to themselves did
they think of me, not about me and what would
become of me—that, in their madness, they never
thought of, as little as they do now, lying there still
and headless, leaving to me what I shall do next! Do?
There is nothing to be done, since now I am undone.
Shall I go through life a widow, shunned as a woman
who cared so ill for her husband that he perished?
That is a widow's common lot; but how much
worse stain will attach to me when I return alone
to the house of my father and my father-in-law?
Only one sword—they cannot have killed each
other with it in turn, one sword is not enough for
two. But there is a third person left, and that is I.
They will say I am an abandoned woman and murdered my husband and his foster-brother, my
brother-in-law—the chain of evidence is complete.
It is false, but it is conclusive and they will brand
me, though innocent. Not innocent, no, there might
be some sense in deceiving oneself, it would be
worth while, if everything were not at an end, but
as it is there is no sense. Innocent I am not, have not
been for long; and as for being abandoned there is
something in it—much, much indeed, though not
quite as people will think. Is there such a thing as
mistaken justice? I must prevent that, I must do

justice on myself. I must follow them—nothing else in the world is left me. The sword I cannot wield with my little hands, they are too small and frightened to destroy the body to which they belong, and these alluring curves—that are yet naught but weakness. A pity for its loveliness—it must become as stiff and lifeless as these, and nevermore awake desire or suffer lust. So must it be, though the number of the sacrifice mount to four. What would it have from life, the orphaned child? Crippled by misfortune, pale and blind because I went pale with affliction when it was conceived, and shut my eyes not to see him who begot it. What I do now is what they have left me to do. Lo, then, let them see I know how to help myself!"

She pulled herself up, staggered to and fro, tottered up the steps, and ran, with her gaze bent on destruction, back through the temple into the open air. A fig tree stood in front of the shrine, hung with climbing vines. She seized one of these, made a noose, put it round her neck, and was just in the act to strangle herself.

8

At that moment a voice was manifest to her out of the air: no other, of course, than the voice of Durga-Devi, the Unapproachable, Kali the dark, the voice of the World-Mother herself. It was a deep, harsh voice, with a maternal firmness about it.

"Will you just let that be for a minute, you silly ape!" it said. "Is it not enough to have let the blood of my sons, so that it flows in the runnels, but you will also mutilate my tree, and make your body—which is not a half-bad image of me—carrion for crows, together with the dear sweet warm little seed of life growing inside it? Perhaps you have not noticed, you goose, that you have missed your times and are in expectation from my son? If you cannot add two and two in women's matters, then hang yourself, do! But not here in my bailiwick, to make it look as though dear life should all at once perish and go out of the world, just on account of your silliness. My ears are full as it is of these quack philosophers who say that human existence is a disease, communicating itself through lust from one generation to the next—and now you, you ninny, start playing games like this with me! Take your neck out of the noose, or you'll get your ears boxed!"

"Holy goddess," answered Sita, "certainly, I obey. I hear the thunder of thy voice and interrupt of course at once my desperate enterprise as thou commandest. But I must defend myself against the idea that I did not realize my condition and not know that you had made me a pause and had blessed me. I only thought it would surely be pale and blind and a child of misfortune."

"Be so good as to let me take care of that! In the first place that is a silly female superstition, and in the second, in my activities there is room for pale and blind cripples too. But justify yourself, confess why the blood of my sons has flowed to me in the pit, both of them in their way very decent chaps. Not that their blood would not have been grateful to me; only I should rather have let it flow awhile yet in their veins. Speak then, but tell the truth! You realize that I know everything anyhow."

"They killed each other, holy goddess, and left me forlorn. They quarrelled on my account and with one and the same sword hewed off their—"

"Nonsense! Really only a female can talk such first-class tripe. They sacrificed themselves to me one after the other in manly piety, let me tell you. But why did they do it?"

The lovely Sita began to weep. She answered sobbing:

"Ah, holy goddess, I know and confess my guilt, but how can I help it? It was such a misfortune, however inevitable; such a fatality, if you don't mind my saying so" (here she sobbed several times); "such a calamity, such poisonous bad luck, that I became a wife, being the pert and tongue-tied and ignorant girl that I was, tending in peace my father's hearth until I knew my husband and was initiated into thy matters. For the blithe child that I was, it was like eating poison berries, changing her for

ever through and through, so that sin, with its irresistible sweetness, has power over her awakened
senses. Not that I can wish myself back in that pert
and unthinking ignorance—I cannot; it is possible
to no one. I only know that in that early time I did
not know man, I did not see him, he did not bother
me, and my soul was free of him and all burning
curiosity about his mysteries; I tossed him jesting
words and went my saucy way. Had ever I blushed
at the sight of a youth's breast or felt my eyes burn
then I looked at his arms and legs? No, all that was
like nothing at all to me, it did not touch ever so
little my coolness and pertness, for I was like a closed
book. A youth came, with a flat nose and black eyes,
pretty as a picture, Nanda was his name, from Welfare of Cows; he swung me up to the sun in the feast
of the sun, but I felt no glow at all. I got hot
—from the caressing air but from nothing else; and
for thanks I gave him a tweak of the nose. Then
he came back as wooer for his friend Shridaman,
and our parents agreed on the marriage. Perhaps by
then it was a little different; perhaps the unhappiness
began in those days when he wooed me for another
man who was to embrace me as his wife and who
was not there. Only Nanda was there.

"He was always there; before the wedding and
during the wedding feast, when we marched round
the fire—and afterwards too. In the daytime, I mean,
he was there, for of course he was not at night,
when I slept with his friend Shridaman, my husband, and we met as the godlike pair as we had for
the first time on the bed of flowers our wedding
night, when he unlocked me with his manly
strength and put an end to my inexperience and the

pert, chaste maidenliness of my early years. That he could do, why not, he was thy son, and he knew how to impart a grace to our physical union, and there was nothing at all against my loving, honouring, and fearing him—ah, most high goddess, I am not so bad, that I should not have loved my lord and husband, and even more feared and honoured him: that head so fine and wise, the beard soft as the soft mild eyes and lids, and the body that went with them. But with all my respect, I had to ask myself whether he was really the right one to make me a wife and instruct my maidenly coldness in the sweet and awful mysteries of sense. —It always seemed to me it did not fit him; it was not worthy of him, it did not go with his head, and always when his flesh rose to encounter me in those wedded nights it seemed to me like a shame, and a degradation of his refinement, a shame and debasement—and for me too when I had been aroused.

"Eternal goddess, so it was. Chide me, punish me, I thy creature confess it all to thee in this frightful hour, saying just how it was; mindful that in any case all things are open to thy wisdom. Desire did not become my noble husband Shridaman, it became neither his head nor his body, which after all, you will agree, is the important factor. His body lying there, so piteously severed from its head, did not know how to shape the rites of love so that my whole heart would hang upon them. He did indeed awake me to desire but could not still it. Have mercy, goddess! The lust of thy awakened creature was greater than its satisfaction, its craving greater than its joy.

"And by day I saw our friend Nanda with the

goat-nose; and in the evening before we went to bed. I saw him and I noticed him, as wedlock had now taught me to see and notice men; and the question slipped into my head and into my dreams: what would Nanda make of the act of love and what would the godlike embrace be like with him—who is very far from talking as well as Shridaman—instead of with my husband? No different, miserable wretch, I told myself, vicious and dishonouring towards thy rightful husband! It is always the same; how could such as Nanda, who is simplicity itself in all his words and members while thy lord and husband is really a person of consequence, how could Nanda know how to make any more of it? But that was no help: the question of Nanda, the idea that his lust would become both his head and his limbs and be without shame, and he might be the man to lift my joy to the level of my desire—it stuck in my flesh and soul like a hook in a fish's mouth, and could not be pulled out because the hook was barbed.

"How could I tear it out, when he was always there, and Shridaman and he could not live without each other because they were so different? I had to see him by day, and dream about him by night, instead of Shridaman. I would look at his breast with the lucky-calf lock, his narrow hips and very small hind-quarters, mine being so large, and Shridaman forming in this respect a mean between me and Nanda, and my self-control forsook me. When his arm touched mine the hairs on my skin rose up for very bliss. When I thought of his glorious pair of legs, with the black hair on them, saw him walk and move them and thought of their clasping me round in

amorous play, a giddiness seized me and my breasts
dripped with tenderness. More and more lovely
he became to me day by day. I could not understand
how I saw him, on the day of my swinging, and
smelt the mustard oil on his skin, and remained
asleep and untouched. For now he was like
the prince Gandharva Citraratha in his unearthly
charm, like the love-god in his sweetest guise, full
of beauty and youth, ravishing to the sense, adorned
with heavenly ornament, with necklaces of flowers,
sweet odours, and all loveliness—Vishnu, come
down to earth in Krishna's form.

"Thus it was, when Shridaman came near me
in the night I paled for very sorrow that it was he
and not the other, and closed my eyes so I might
think Nanda embraced me. It came about that I
forbore not, in my ardour, to murmur the name of
him whom I would have wished to rouse it in me;
and so Shridaman became aware that I was breaking my marriage vows in his gentle arms. And then,
alas, I sometimes talk in my sleep, and I must have
hurt him cruelly by uttering within his hearing the
betraying substance of my dreams. I gather this
from his melancholy and his withdrawal from me—
for from that time he has never touched me again.
Nor did Nanda touch me; not because he was not
tempted, tempted he certainly was, I would swear
to it that he was sorely tempted! But in his invincible
loyalty to his friend he resisted the temptation, and
I too—believe me, eternal Mother, for I at least do
believe it—even if his temptation had mastered
him, out of honour for my lord and husband I would
have showed him the door. But the issue was that I

had no husband at all; and the three of us were in a state of painful renunciation.

"Under such circumstances, Mother of the world, we undertook the journey to my parents and wandering from our right ways we came on thy house. Shridaman said he would stop only a little and in passing pay you his devotions. But in thy slaughter-cell, overcome by his plight, he did this frightful deed, robbing his limbs of their revered head, or rather his revered head of its limbs, and abandoned me to this wretched widowed state. In an agony of abnegation he did it, and with good intentions towards me, the criminal. For, gracious goddess, pardon me the truth: not to thee did he bring himself a sacrifice but to me and to his friend, that we might spend our days in full enjoyment of the joys of the flesh. Then Nanda went to seek him, and would not abide by the sacrifice but hacked his own head from his Krishna limbs, so that they are now useless. But useless, yes, and much worse than useless my life is now become; I too am as good as headless, without husband or friend. The guilt for my unhappiness I must, I suppose, ascribe to my acts in a former existence. But after all this, canst thou wonder that I was resolved to make an end of my present one?"

"You are an unqualified goose, and nothing else," said the goddess in her voice of thunder. "It is ridiculous, what your insatiable curiosity has made out of this Nanda, who is entirely ordinary in all his works and ways. With such arms, and on such legs, I have sons running about by the million, and you go and make a Gandharva out of him! It is pathetic, after all," added the divine voice more mildly. "I, the Mother, find fleshly lust pathetic on the whole, and am of opinion that people are inclined to make too much of it. Anyhow, order there must be!" And the voice got suddenly harsh and blustering again. "I, indeed, am Disorder; but precisely therefore I insist on order, and I must definitely protest that the institution of marriage be kept inviolate. Everything would get into a muddle if I gave rein to my good nature. But as for you, to say I am dissatisfied is to put it mildly. You make this kettle of fish for me here and on the top of it you say all sorts of impudent things to me. You give me to understand that my sons did not offer themselves as sacrifices that their blood might flow to my altar—you say the first sacrificed himself to you, and then the second to the first. What kind of manners are those? How could a man hew off his head—not simply cut his throat but cut off his head according to the proper rites (and an educated man to boot, like your Shridaman, who doesn't show up so well in the business of love)—unless he got the necessary strength and wildness out of the intoxication that came to him from me? So I forbid your tone, quite aside from whether there is any truth in your words or not! For there may be truth in them, in so far that a deed has been committed with mixed motives, and is so far unclear. It was not exclusively to seek my mercy that my son Shridaman offered himself up; actually it was for affliction about you, whether he himself was clear in the matter or no. And little Nanda's sacrifice was just the inevitable consequence. I feel little inclined to receive their blood and accept the offering. Well then:

if I now make good the double sacrifice and put all
back as it was, may I be permitted to hope that
you will behave with more decency in the future?"

"Ah, holy goddess and dear Mother!" cried
Sita through her tears. "If you could do that, if you
could cancel these frightful deeds and give me back
husband and friend so that all were as before—how
would I bless you! I would even control my dreams
and the words of them so that the noble Shridaman
need suffer no more. Indescribably thankful would
I be to you, if you brought that about and put everything back as it was! For though it was sad enough
before, and when I stood there in your Innermost
before the kettle of fish, I realized clear and plain
that it could not have turned out otherwise, yet
it would be wonderful if you had the power and
could succeed in reversing the past so that next time
it might have a better issue."

"What do you mean by 'if I had the power'
and 'if I could succeed'?" retorted the divine voice.
"I hope you do not doubt that to my power it were
the merest trifle! More than once in the world it has
come to pass that I showed it. But I am sorry for
you, I must say, although you do not deserve it, you
and the pale, blind little seedling in your womb.
The two young men in there, I pity them too. So
open your ears and hear what I tell you! Drop that
vegetable choker of yours and get back with you
into my shrine, before my image and the mess you
have made. No fainting or whimpering, mind! You
take the two heads by the hair and fit them to the
poor trunks again. Then you bless the cuts with the
sharp edge of the sword of sacrifice, and both times
call upon my name—you may say Durga or Kali

or simply Devi, it doesn't matter—and the two youths will be restored to life. Do you understand me? Do not approach the heads too quickly to the bodies, although you will feel strong attraction between head and trunk; the spilt blood must have time to run back and be sucked in again. That happens with magic quickness, but after all it takes a moment of time. I hope you have listened to me? Then run! But do the trick properly, do not put the heads on wrong way round in your flurry so that they have to go about with their faces backwards and make people laugh at them! Get along! If you wait till tomorrow it will be too late."

9

The lovely Sita said nothing more at all, not even "thank you"; she jumped up and ran, fast as her swathed robe would let her, back into the mother-house. She ran through the audience chamber and through the entrance hall and into the holy shrine, and there before the frightful countenance of the goddess she set to the prescribed task with flushed and feverish energy. The attraction between heads and trunks was not so strong as one might have expected from Devi's words. It was perceptible; but yet there was time for the blood to flow back up the channels, as it did with magical swiftness and a lively lapping sound. The blessing of the sword infallibly performed its office—that and the divine name which Sita, her voice breaking with joy, cried out three times in each case. Each with his head in its place, without mark or scar the youths rose before her. They looked at her and down at themselves—or rather, in so going they looked at each other; for to look at themselves they had to look over at each other, such being the nature of their restoration.

Sita, what has thou done? Or what has happened? Or what in thy flurry hast thou made to happen? In a word (to put the question so that it takes proper cognizance of the fluid boundary between doing and happening), what has come to pass with you? The excitement in which you acted is understandable; but could you not have opened

your eyes a little better while you did it? No, you
did not put back the heads the wrong way round—
this did not happen at all. But—to tell it straight
out and call the amazing truth by its name—the
mischance, the mistake, the kettle of fish, or whatever all three of you might feel like calling it, that
confronted you was this: you have fitted on to each
one and sealed fast with the sword the other's head.
Nanda's to Shridaman—if we may call his trunk
without the chief feature of it Shridaman at all—and
Shridaman's to Nanda, if the headless Nanda was
in fact still Nanda. In short, they arose before you,
not husband and friend in their order, but mixed
together. You behold Nanda—if he is Nanda, who
wears Nanda's nice little head atop—in the smock
and draped trousers enveloping Shridaman's plump,
slender-limbed body. You behold Shridaman—if
the form may be so named that is equipped with his
mild and gentle headpiece—standing before you on
Nanda's well-shaped legs, the lucky-calf lock
framed in stone-pearls on "his" broad bronze chest!

What a state of things—all in consequence of
too much flurry! They lived who had been sacrifices. But they lived transformed; the body of the
husband dwelt with the head of his friend, the body
of the friend with the husband's head. No wonder
that the rocky cave echoed and reechoed as the
three prolonged their amazed outcry! The one with
the Nanda-head felt all down the limbs and body
which once had been appended, a mere detail, to
the noble head of Shridaman; while that Shridaman
(if we take the head as the decisive factor) stood
full of embarrassment, seeking to recognize as his
own the body which—when Nanda's simple head

sat on its shoulders—had been the essential feature. As for the moving cause of this new order of things, she went from one to the other by turns, with cries of joy, with loud wailing and remorse; embraced first one and then the other, and at last threw herself at their feet to confess between sobs and laughter all that had happened and the late lamentable oversight.

"Forgive me, if you can!" she cried. "Forgive me, dear Shridaman"—and she turned expressly to his head, deliberately overlooking the Nanda-body it sat on—"forgive me too, Nanda"—again she spoke to the head in question as the essential thing, regarding it, despite its insignificance, as important and the Shridaman-body thereto attached as the indifferent appendage. "Oh, you ought to be able to forgive me! Think of the frightful deed to which as you then were you persuaded yourselves, and the despair into which you flung me. Realize that I was about to strangle myself and after that had speech with the Unapproachable and heard her voice of thunder, which almost robbed me of my senses! Then you can realize that I was hardly in a frame to carry out her commands. Things swam before my eyes, I saw only unclearly whose head and limbs I had in my hands and had to trust to luck that the right would find the right. Half the chances were for it, and half against—and it has just turned out this way, and you have come out like this. How could I know whether the power of attraction between head and limbs was in the right proportion, when it was clear and strong as it was, though of course in different combination it might have been even more so? And the Unapproachable must bear

some of the blame too; for she only warned me not
to put your heads on wrong side before, and that I
was careful about; that it could come out as it has,
the high goddess never thought of that! Tell me,
are you in despair over the manner of your resur-
rection and will you curse me for ever? If so, I will
go and carry out the deed in which I was interrupted
by her that was before all beginnings. Or are you
inclined to forgive me, can you find it possible that
under these circumstances brought about by blind
chance, a new and better life could begin between
us three—a better one, I mean, than would have
been possible if the former situation were just restored as it was and by all human calculations must
have had just the same sad issue again? Tell me,
Shridaman of the powerful limbs! Slender Nanda,
let me hear!"

Vying in pardon, the transformed youths bent
over, lifted her up, the one with the other's arms,
and all three stood embraced, weeping and laughing together. Two things became at once very clear;
first, that Sita had been quite right in addressing
the resurrected friends according to their heads;
for it was definitely by these that their I- and my-
feelings were conditioned. He who on narrow, light-
complexioned shoulders bore the simple head of
Garga's son knew himself to be Nanda. And equally
the other, with the head of the grandson of Brahmans on top of a broad, bronze-coloured frame,
knew and comported himself as Shridaman. But
secondly, it was manifest that neither of them was
angry at Sita for her mistake, but both actually
found pleasure in their new guise.

"If Nanda," said Shridaman, "is not ashamed of

the body that has fallen to his lot, and does not miss too much the breast-lock of Krishna, which would be painful to me, for myself I can only say that I count myself the happiest of men. I have always wished I could have a bodily form like this; when I feel the muscles of my arms, look at my shoulders and down at my magnificent legs, I am seized with unrestrained delight, and say to myself that from now on I shall hold my head high, in quite a new way; first in the consciousness of my new strength and beauty, and second because my spiritual lean-ings will now be in harmony with my physical build, and it will no longer be wrong or unfitting for me to speak in favour of simplification and cast my vote under the tree for the procession of cows round the mountain Bright Peak instead of for the Brahmanical rites, for it has become quite right and proper and what was foreign to me is so no more. Of course, my dear friends, there is a certain sad-ness in this, that the strange is now become my own and no longer an object of desire and admiration, except that I admire myself and that I no longer serve something else in choosing the mountain feast instead of the Indra-feast, but rather that which I myself am. Yes—this kind of sadness, due to my now being that towards which I once yearned, I feel it, I admit. But it retreats into the background at the thought of you, sweet Sita, for you come be-fore all thought of myself, and the advantage you will reap from my new circumstances—of which I am even now so proud and glad that for my part I can only bless this whole miracle and say: Siya, be it so!"

"You might at least be correct and say Siyat,"

said Nanda, whose eyes at his friend's last words had sought the ground, "instead of letting your peasant limbs rule your mouth. You are welcome to them, so far as I am concerned, I have had them much too long. But neither am I angry with you, Sita. I, too, say Siyat to this miracle, for I have always wanted a slender body like this, and now, when I speak for Indra's cult of words and against simplification, it will become me better than it did before —or at least if not my face it will become my body, which is now a minor matter to you, Shridaman, but to me it is the main point. I am not at all surprised that our heads and bodies, when you put them together, Sita, displayed such strong attraction; it was the power of the friendship which bound Shridaman and me, and of which I can only hope it may suffer no breach through what has happened. But one thing I may say: my poor head cannot help thinking for the body that has fallen to its lot, and seeing where its rights lie; and therefore I am astonished and dismayed at certain of Shridaman's words and the way they took Sita's future for granted. I see nothing here that can be taken for granted. There is only a very great question, and my head answers it otherwise than yours seems to."

"How so?" cried Sita and Shridaman as with one voice.

"How so?" repeated the slender-limbed friend. "How can you even ask? To me my body is the main point, and in this I conform to the idea of marriage, for with the body are children begot and not with the head. I should like to see him who would deny that I am the father of the fruit Sita bears in her womb."

"Pull your wits together, Nanda!" cried Shri-daman, with an involuntary shift of his powerful limbs, "and think what you are saying. Are you Nanda, or who are you?"

"I am Nanda," the other replied. "But as truly as I call this wedded body mine and use the word 'I' of it, just so truly is Sita of the lovely curves my wife and her fruit of my begetting."

"Indeed!" retorted Shridaman, with a quiver in his voice. "Is it really? I should not have dared to assert it, when your present body was still mine and slept at Sita's side. For it was not that body she really embraced, as I learned to my sorrow when she muttered in her sleep. Instead it was the one I now call my own. It is not in good taste, my friend, for you to touch on these painful matters and force me to speak of them. How can you insist on your head like this, or rather on your body, and behave as though you had become I, and I you? Surely it is clear that if that kind of exchange had taken place and you had become Shridaman, Sita's husband, and I Nanda, then there would be no change at all, and everything would be as it had been. The happy mir-acle is that only an exchange of heads and limbs has come about at Sita's hands, whereat our heads rejoice, being the decisive factor. Above all, our re-joicing is due to the happiness in store for Sita of the lovely hips. But now here you are, obstinately pre-suming on your present body, which is that of a married man, and assigning to me the rôle of friend! You display a culpable egotism, for you are think-ing only of yourself and not at all of how she will profit by the change."

"She would profit, as you call it," retorted Nanda, not without bitterness, "from advantages you are now proud to call your own. You are just as egotistic as I am. And you misunderstand me besides. I do not refer to this married body I now have, but to my very own proper head, which you yourself declare to be decisive, making me Nanda even when connected with my new and finer body. You are wrong to say I am not at least as mindful of Sita as you are. When she looked at me of late—speaking in her sweetly trilling and lilting voice, which I feared to hear lest I should answer in the same tone—she looked into my face and into my eyes, seeking to read therein with her own, calling me Nanda and dear Nanda. At the time it seemed unnecessary, but I now see it had great spiritual significance. It showed that she did not mean my body, which in and of itself does not deserve the name; you yourself have proved that, for now that you have it you still call yourself Shridaman. I did not reply to her, except for the most necessary things, and scarcely those, so as not to fall into the same trilling and thrilling key. I did not call her by name, I kept my eyes down so she could not read in them—all out of friendship for you and reverence for your wedded state. But now I have not only the head and the eyes she gazed into so deep and questioningly, saying 'Nanda' and 'oh, dear Nanda'; but the husband-body as well—and the situation is fundamentally changed in mine and Sita's favour. Hers above all! For if we are to put her happiness and satisfaction before everything else, then certainly there can be no purer and more perfect solution than the one I describe."

"No," said Shridaman, "I would not have ex-

pected this from you. I was afraid lest you might be
ashamed of my body; but now my former body
might blush for your head, in such contradictions
do you involve yourself, arbitrarily taking now the
head and now the body as the important thing in
marriage! You have always been a modest youth;
but now all at once you scale the heights of pre-
sumption, and declare your situation the purest and
perfectest in the world to guarantee Sita's happiness,
when it is obvious that it is I who have the best,
that is to say at once the happiest and most reassuring possible. But there is no sense or purpose in talking further. Here stands Sita. She must say to whom
she belongs and be the judge of us and her own
happiness."

Sita looked bewildered from one to the other.
Then she buried her face in her hands and wept.

"I cannot," she sobbed. "Do not force me to decide, I am only a poor female, it is too hard for me.
At first, it seemed quite easy, and however ashamed
I was of my mistake, yet I was happy about it, especially when I saw you were both happy too. But
your words have bewildered my brain and cleft my
heart in twain, so that one half opposes the other
half as you do each other. In your words, dear Shridaman, there is much truth, and you have not even
brought it up that I can only go home with a husband who wears your features. But Nanda's opinion too I sympathize with; when I remember how
pathetic and insignificant his body looked without
its head, I must agree with him that I probably
meant his head more than his body when I said 'dear
Nanda' to him. But you used the word 'reassuring,'
dear Shridaman; and it is difficult indeed to say

whether the head or the body of my husband would
reassure me more. Do not torture me! I am quite
incapable of solving the riddle, I have no power to
judge which of you is my husband."

"If matters stand so," said Nanda, after a helpless silence, "and Sita cannot decide and judge between us, then judgement must come from a third
or rather from a fourth party. When Sita just now
said that she can only go home with a man who
wears Shridaman's features, then I thought in my
own mind that she and I would not go home but
live somewhere in retirement, in case she should
find a reassuring life with me as her husband. The
thought of solitude in the wilderness has long been
attractive to me, for when Sita's voice made me
doubt the loyalty of my friendship, I would think
that perhaps I might become a hermit. And I made
acquaintance with such a man, practised in self-
mortification, Kamadamana by name, that he might
give me instruction in that kind of life. I visited
him in the Dankaka forest where he lives, and where
there are very many other holy men all about. His
family name is just Guha; but he took the religious
name of Kamadamana, by which he desires to be
called—so far as anybody has a chance to call him
anything. For many years he has lived in the Dankaka forest with strict vows concerning bathing and
speaking. I should say he cannot be far from his
transfiguration. Let us go to this wise man, who
knows and has vanquished life. Let us tell him our
story and put him as judge over Sita's happiness.
Let him decide, if you are agreed, which of us two
is her husband, and may his words prevail."

"Yes, yes," cried Sita with relief, "Nanda is right, let us get up and go to the holy man."

"I see," said Shridaman, "that what we have here is an objective problem not to be solved from within but only by outward wisdom; I agree to the suggestion and am ready to submit to the judgement of the wise man."

Being now so far agreed, they left the mother-house together and returned to their conveyance standing down in the gulley. Here the question arose which of the friends should drive, that being a matter of the body and the head both. Nanda, of course, knew the way to the Dankaka forest, which was two days' journey away. He had it all in his head; while Shridaman was now better adapted to hold the reins, just as Nanda had been before. He gave up the office to Shridaman and sat down behind him with Sita; but prompted his friend on the way he should take.

10

On the third day they reached the Dankaka forest, which was green with the rains and thickly populated with holy men, though large enough to afford each one sufficient seclusion and his own grim little holding void of human kind. It was not easy for the pilgrims to question their way through from solitude to solitude and find Kamadamana, the vanquisher of desires. All the hermits were one in wishing to know nothing of each other and each protested his conviction that he was alone in the wood, surrounded by his own unpeopled void. Holy men of various degrees were here: some of them had passed the stage of householder, and now, sometimes accompanied by their wives, were devoting the remainder of their lives to a mild form of contemplativeness. Others were yogi of the thick and thin kind, so to speak: they had as good as completely bridled the steeds of sense, by mortification and abstention fought their flesh to the knife, and managed to carry through the most awful vows. They fasted to the point of death; slept naked in the rain on the ground, and in the cold season wore their clothing wet. In the summer they lay between four fire-brands to consume their earthly flesh—in part it dripped from them, in part was consumed in the parching heat. To this they added further discipline by rolling days at a time on the ground, or stood continuously on the tips of their toes, or kept in constant motion by standing up and sitting down in quick succession. If by such practices they injured their health and the approach of their apotheosis was indicated, then they set forth on their final pilgrimage due north and east, taking neither herbs nor roots to their nourishment but only water and air, until their bodies gave way and their souls were united with Brahma.

The seekers after decision encountered these various kinds as they wandered through the holdings of successive solitaries, having first left their conveyance at the edge of the woods with a hermit family they found leading a relatively light-minded life there, in touch to some extent with the outer world. The path to the particular unpeopled void where Kamadamana dwelt was, as we said, hard to find. True, Nanda had once already found the way thither through the trackless waste. But he had done so in another body, and this hampered his intuition and sense of locality. The denizens of the caves and hollow trees were either ignorant or pretended to be so. It was only with the help of the wives of some former householders who behind the backs of their lords goodheartedly pointed out the way, and after another whole day and night spent in the wilderness, that they arrived in the preserve of their particular saint, and saw his whitewashed head with its sausage of braided hair, and his arms like dried branches reared up heavenwards, rising out of a swampy pool where he had been standing, God knows how long, up to his neck in water, his spirit gathered to a fine point. They refrained from calling to him out of reverence for so much burning zeal, and waited patiently for him to intermit his discipline. However

he did not do so for a long time; either because he
had not seen them or else just because he had. They
had to wait for as much as an hour, keeping a modest distance from the pool, before he came out, quite
naked, his beard and his body hair dripping with
mud. His body was as good as fleshless, consisting
merely of skin and bones; so there was, in a manner
of speaking, nothing at all to his nakedness. As he
approached the waiting group he swept the ground
before his feet with a broom which he had taken
from the bank. This, they knew, was in order not
to crush any living creature that might be there. But
he was not nearly so gentle to his unbidden guests:
for as he came on he threatened them with uplifted
broom, heedless that something irretrievable might
happen to the creeping and crawling things where
he trod, and that theirs would be the blame.

"Away," he shouted, "ye idlers and gapers!
What seek ye in my unpeopled void?"

"O Kamadamana, vanquisher of desire," answered Nanda with due modesty, "forgive us that
in our need we have so boldly approached you!
The fame of your self-conquest has tempted us
hither, driven by the urges of this fleshly life. Deign
then, O bull among wise men, to give us advice
and useful counsel. Pray be so good as to remember me! Once already have I confided in you, to
partake of your wisdom on the subject of the
solitary life."

"It is possible that I may recognize you," said
the recluse, looking at Nanda out of the deep caverns
of his eyes, from under their threatening thatch of
brow. "At least I might recognize your face; but
your form seems in the meantime to have gone

through a certain refining process which I suppose
I may ascribe to your former visit."

"It did me a great deal of good," Nanda
answered evasively. "But the change you perceive
has a different cause and belongs to a story full of
strangeness and stress, which is precisely the story
of us three who petition you. It has set us face to
face with a question we cannot solve by ourselves;
we must obtain your advice and judgement. We
have hope that your self-conquest may be so great
that you can bring yourself to hearken to us."

"It shall be," answered Kamadamana. "No one
shall say that it would not. Of course it was my first
impulse to chase you out of my preserve; but that
too was an impulse which I reject and a temptation
I am minded to resist. For if it is self-denial to avoid
men, it is still greater self-denial to put up with
them. Trust me, your nearness and the fumes of life
you give out lie heavy on my chest and bring an
unpleasant flush to my cheek, as you could see were
it not for their seemly coating of ashes. But I
am ready to bear with you and your vapours, particularly since I have observed from the first that
among the three of you is a woman grown, whom
the senses find glorious; slender as a vine, with soft
thighs and full breasts, oh yea, oh fie! Her navel is
beauteous, her face lovely with partridge-eyes, and
her breasts, I repeat, are full and upstanding. Good-
day, O woman! When men look upon you, do not
the hairs of their bodies rise up for lust? And the
troubles of the three of you, are they not all due to
you, you snare and allurement? Hail! I should most
likely have sent these young men to the devil, but
since you are with them, my dear, pray stay, stop

as long as you like! I rejoice to invite you to my hollow tree, where I will regale you with the jujube berries I have gathered there in leaves, not to eat but to fast from, and with them in my sight gnaw roots instead, since this earthly frame must from time to time be fed. And I will listen to your tale, though the fumes of life it exhales will come nigh to choke me. Word for word will I listen to it, for no one shall ever tax Kamadamana with lack of courage. True, it is hard to distinguish between courage and curiosity. It might be that I listen to you because I have got hungry here in my retreat, and lustful to have the fumes of real life in my nostrils. But the idea must be rejected, and no less the further suggestion that curiosity here too acts to prompt the rejection and nip it in the bud, so that actually it is the curiosity that ought to be nipped. But if so, then what about my courage? It is the same as it is with the jujube berries. The thought probably tempts me that I keep them beside me not so much to renounce them as to enjoy the sight of them. To which I courageously reply that the pleasure of looking at them constitutes the temptation to eat them. Thus I should make life too easy for myself if I did not keep them beside me. And so the suspicion is done away with, that I have thought up this answer just for the sake of being able to share the alluring sight—since, even if I do not eat the berries myself but give them to you to eat, I can enjoy seeing you put them down. And that, in view of the illusory character of the divers manifestations on this earth, and of any distinction between the I and the you, is almost the same as though I ate them myself. In short, asceticism is a bottomless vat; because the temptations of the spirit are mingled therein with the temptations of the flesh, until the whole thing is like the snake that grows two heads as soon as you cut off one. But it is all quite right, and after all the main thing is to have courage. So come with me, you life-reeking mortals of both sexes, come with me to my hollow tree and tell me of all life's manifold uncleanlinesses; tell me as much as you like, and I will listen, for my correction and to get rid of the idea that I am doing it for my own entertainment—the more one gets rid of, the better!"

With these words the holy man led the way for some distance through the jungle, always carefully sweeping before him with his broom. And they arrived at his own place, a huge, very old kadamba tree, still green though it was only a gaping hollow inside. Kamadamana had chosen this mossy, earthy home not for protection against the weather, for he constantly exposed his frame to it, abetting the heat with firebrands and the cold with wetness. No, it was only that he might know where he belonged, and have a place to store his supply of roots, tubers, and fruits to eat, and firewood, flowers, and grasses for offerings.

Here he bade his guests sit down, which they hastened to do, in all modesty, well knowing that they were here only for his asceticism, so to speak, to sharpen its teeth on. He gave them the jujube berries as he had promised and they were no little refreshed. He himself meanwhile assumed an ascetic attitude, which is called the Kajotsarga position: with motionless limbs, arms directed stiffly downwards, and rigid knee-joints. He contrived to keep separate, somehow or other, not only his fingers but his toes as well; and thus remained, his spirit gathered to a point, in all his nakedness, which signified so very little because of the lack of flesh. To Shridaman, because of his headpiece, the office of narrator had fallen; so he stood in all the magnificence of his present form beside the other, and spoke of the events which had brought them hither and the vexed question which could only be solved by a fourth party, as some saint or king.

He told it truthfully, as we have told it, in part in the same words. To make clear the disputed point, it would have been enough to tell only the final stage. But he reported it from the beginning just as it happened, in order to give the holy man a little treat in his unpeopled void. He began with an account of Nanda's life and his own, the friendship between them, and the way they broke their journey at the river Goldfly. He described his love-sickness, his wooing and marriage, weaving in such earlier information as Nanda's swinging acquaintance with Sita. Other points, such as the bitter experiences of his married life, he touched on with delicacy or only by inference, not to spare himself, since his were now the stout arms that had swung Sita up to the sun, and his the living body of which she had dreamed in his former arms. No, it was out of regard for Sita herself, for whom none of this could be very pleasant and who throughout the narrative kept her little head shrouded in her embroidered scarf.

The powerful Shridaman, thanks to his headpiece, proved a good and skilful narrator. Even Sita and Nanda, who knew the whole thing, of course, heard their own story all over again, horrible as it was, with pleasure from his lips, and Kamadamana, although he maintained his Kajotsarga position unmoved, presumably found it arresting too. Shridaman recounted his own and Nanda's grisly deed, the relenting of the goddess to Sita, and Sita's pardonable error at the work of restoration. At last he got to the end, and put the question.

"Thus and thus," said he, "the husband's head was bestowed on the body of his friend, the friend's on the body of the husband. Be so gracious, then, as to pronounce in your wisdom upon our bewildered state, holy Kamadamana! As you decree, so will we be bound and act according, for we ourselves cannot decide. To whom now belongs this all-round fine-limbed woman, and who is truly her husband?"

"Yes, tell us, tell us, O vanquisher of desire!" cried Nanda loudly and with confidence. Sita only hastily pulled her veil from her head to direct her lotus-eyes expectantly upon Kamadamana.

The latter drew his fingers and toes together and sighed deeply. Then he took his broom, swept himself a spot on the ground free from vulnerable insects, and sat down with his guests.

"Faugh!" said he. "You three are certainly the right people for me! I was prepared of course for a tale of life's headiest fumes. But this of yours, you could fairly cut it with a knife. It is easier for me to hold out between my four fire-brands in the hottest summer heat than to breathe in the steam you are giving out. If I had not rouged my face with ashes you could see the flush on my decently lank cheeks or rather on the ascetic bones of them. Ah, children, children! Like to the ox that with his eyes bound up turns the oil-mill round and round, so you are turned upon the wheel of life, anguished with appetite, pricked and twitched in your flesh by the six miller's men of the passions. Could you not leave off? Must you still go on, with your ogling, licking, slavering, your knees giving way with desire when the object of your delusion heaves in sight? Yes, yes, I know, I know it all: the body of love, with bitter lust bedewed—limb-play neath satin skin, unguent-imbrued—the graceful vault the shoulder makes—the sniffing nose, loose mouth that seeks—sweet breasts adorned with tender stars—the arm-pits' hollows with sweat-drenchèd beards—oh, pasturage for hands to rove, fair hips, fine loins, back supple, belly breathing love—the bliss-embrace of arms, the bloomy thighs, cool twin delight of hillocks that behind them lies—till all agog with lust at pitch they work at coupling play in hot and reeking dark, each urging other on more bliss to capture, they flute each other to a heaven of rapture—and this and that and here and there—I know it all, of all I am aware!"

"But so are we—we know all that ourselves and by ourselves, great Kamadamana," said Nanda with suppressed impatience in his voice. "Will you not be so good as to come to the point and instruct us, who is Sita's husband, that we may finally know and act according?"

"The judgement," replied the holy man, "is as good as given. It is so clear that I am surprised you are not far enough along in knowledge of the right things that you need a judge in so clear and self-evident a matter. The little tidbit there, of course, is the wife of him who has the friend's head on his shoulders. For in marriage one reaches the right hand to the bride; but the hand belongs to the body; and the body is the friend's."

With an exultant cry Nanda leaped to his finely shaped feet. Sita and Shridaman sat still with bowed heads.

"But that is only the premise," Kamadamana went on in a louder voice. "The conclusion follows to outmount and outsound till with truth it is crowned. Please wait a moment."

With that he stood up and went inside his hollow, fetched a rough garment, a sort of apron made out of thin bark, and clothed his nakedness with it. Then he spoke:

> "Husband is, who wears the husband's head.
> Here lies no doubt at all, must it be said,
> As woman is the highest bliss and bourne
>   of songs,
> So among limbs to head the highest rank
>   belongs."

It was Sita's and Shridaman's turn to lift their heads and look joyfully at each other. Nanda, who had but now been so glad, remarked in a crestfallen voice:

"But you said it quite differently before!"

"What I said last," replied Kamadamana, "that goes."

So now they had their verdict. Nanda, in his refined state, could least of all murmur against it, since he himself had proposed to take the holy man

for their judge. Nor could he object to the ir-
reproachable gallantry on which Kamadamana had
based his decree.

They all bowed low before Kamadamana and
departed hence. Together they went, not speaking,
for some distance through the Dankaka forest, green
with the rains. Then Nanda stopped in his tracks and
took leave of them.

"All the best to you," said he. "I will now go
my ways. I will find me an unpeopled void and become a hermit, as I meant to before. Anyway, in
my present incorporation I feel myself a little too
good for the world."

Neither of them could blame him for his decision. They agreed with him, though it made them
feel slightly depressed; and bade him farewell with
the friendliness one shows towards a man who has
drawn the shorter straw. Shridaman clapped him
encouragingly on the so familiar shoulder and ad-
vised him, with a concern such as one seldom feels
for anybody else, not to plague his body with extravagant discipline, and not to eat too many tubers,
for he knew that a monotonous diet did not suit
him.

"Let that be my affair," said Nanda ungra-
ciously. And when Sita tried to utter words of con-
solation he only shook his goat-nosed head, in bitter
melancholy.

"Don't take it so to heart," said she. "Don't for-
get that you nearly won out, and that you might
be now about to share with me the legal couch in
nights of bliss. Be sure I shall always enfold in sweetest tenderness from one end to the other all that
once was yours, and with hand and lips show grati-

tude for my joy, in ways so delectable that only the eternal Mother can teach them to me!"

"Of all that I shall have nothing," he replied obstinately. She even whispered to him: "Sometimes I will put your head on in my dreams too"; but his mien did not change, he only said sadly and stubbornly: "Of that I shall have nothing."

So they parted, the one and the two. But Sita turned back when Nanda was already a little distant, and flung her arms about him.

"Farewell," said she. "After all, you were my first husband, you first awakened me and taught me love so far as I know it; and whatever that dried-up saint may say and sing about wives and heads, the fruit beneath my heart comes from you after all!"

With that she ran back to Shridaman the stout-bodied.

Once back at Welfare of Cows, Sita and Shridaman spent their days and nights in full enjoyment
of the pleasures of sense; nor did any shadow trouble
at first the cloudless heaven of their bliss. The little
words "at first," a faint premonitory troubling of
their unclouded sky, are an addition by one nar-
rating the story from outside and passing on it;
whereas they who lived in it, whose story it is, knew
of no "at first," but were only aware of their joy,
which on both sides must be considered no common
thing.

It was, indeed, a happiness such as belongs to
paradise and seldom to this earth. The common
earthly joys, the gratifications falling to the lot of
mortals in all the conditions of the moral order and
social pressure under which we live, are circum-
scribed indeed. Makeshifts, renunciations, and res-
ignation are the common lot. Our desires are bound-
less, their fulfilment sharply restricted; "If I only
could" is met on all sides by the stern "It won't do."
Life soberly bids us put up with what we can get.
A few things are granted, but more denied; that
they will one day be granted is and remains a dream.
A paradisial dream, of course; for in paradise, surely,
that which is forbidden and that which is granted,
so diverse here below, must there become one. The
lovely forbidden must be crowned with legality,
while the legal attains to all the charms of the for-

bidden. For in what other guise can paradise appear to the hankering man?

Well, it was just this unearthly kind of happiness that a capricious fate had dealt out to the wedded lovers on their return to Welfare of Cows. They drank it down in drunken gulps—at first. For Sita, the awakened, lover and friend had been two different people; but now, oh joy, they were one, and—as it turned out, and could not have turned out differently—the best of each. What had been the main thing in each had joined to form a new individuality surpassing all desire. Nightly on her lawful couch she nestled in the stout arms of Shridaman's friend and experienced his raptures as once on her husband's tender bosom she had closed her eyes and dreamed of them. Yet it was the headpiece of the descendant of Brahmans that she kissed in gratitude—the most highly favoured woman in all the world, for she possessed a husband who, so to speak, consisted of nothing but principal features.

And Shridaman, the transformed husband—how proud and glad was he not in his turn! We need not be concerned lest the change in him made an unpleasant impression on Bhavabhuti his father or on his mother (whose name does not occur in the story because she plays so modest a rôle) or on any other member of the Brahman merchant's family or the other inhabitants of the temple village. The idea that there was anything wrong or unnatural about Shridaman's physical improvement (as though the natural things were the only right ones!) might more easily have arisen, if the metamorphosed Nanda had been there too. But he was far away, leading

the hermit life, to which he had previously sometimes showed a leaning. The change in him, which
might have been striking when viewed together
with his friend's, was known to nobody; there was
only Shridaman, whose bronzed and beauteous
limbs might be credited (so far as they were noticed
at all) to the beneficial effect of married life on his
masculine development. Sita's lord and husband, of
course, did not go about in Nanda's loincloth, arm-
bands, and stone-pearl necklace. Conformably to
his headpiece, he wore as before the draped trousers
and cotton smock which had always been his garb.
And in this we must see undeniable proof of the
contention that the head is the all-important factor
in establishing the human being's identity. Try to
imagine your son or your brother or some fellow-
citizen entering the room with his perfectly well-
known head on his shoulders; whatever might be out
of order with the rest of his appearance, would you
entertain the smallest doubt that this was actually
the brother, son, or fellow-citizen in question?

The description of Sita's bliss has been given
precedence over Shridaman's in this narrative just
as he himself, directly after his transformation,
placed it, as we saw, before his own. But his happiness was in fact equal to hers and wore the same
paradisial face. Indeed, I cannot sufficiently adjure
the listener to put himself in Shridaman's place.
Here was a lover who had shrunk in profound de-
jection from the beloved object, being driven to
realize that she longed for the embraces of another.
And now he was in the incomparable position of
offering her everything she had so mortally craved.
One feels tempted to rank his good fortune above

that of the charming Sita. That love for Sumantra's
golden child that had seized upon Shridaman when
he saw her at her ritual bath—a love so deep and
ardent that he had thought he must die of it, to the
great amusement of Nanda's vulgar mind; that violent, anguished attack of tenderness, kindled by a
lovely image on which he at once hastened to con-
fer a human dignity; that rapture, in short, born,
of course, of spirit and sense combined, and of his
whole personality—had been above all and in es-
sentials a matter of his Brahman head, gifted by the
goddess Speech with fervour of thought and power
of imagination. That head's mild appendage, Shridaman's body, was no equal partner to it, and must
in the marriage relation have betrayed the fact.
Can we now realize the joy, the satisfaction of such
a being, when to such a gifted, ardent, subtle head
was added a good, gay ordinary body, a body simple
and strong, adequate to the spiritual passions conceived in the head? It is idle to imagine the blisses
of paradise—in other words, life in the pleasure-
grove called Joy—otherwise than in the image of
this perfection.

Even the depressing "at first" does not come in,
up there, and indeed makes no real difference, since
it is not in the consciousness of those concerned, but
belongs solely to the controlling sphere of the narrator's mind and thus casts only an objective, im-
personal shadow. But now, indeed, it must be told
that very soon, very early, it began to glide into
the personal sphere; yes, probably from the beginning it played its earthly rôle to limit and condition in a way surely unknown in paradise. We
must admit that Sita of the lovely hips had made a

mistake when she carried out in the way she did the goddess's gracious command: a mistake not only in so far as she carried it out in blind haste, but also in so far as she carried it out not quite and altogether in blind haste. This sentence has been well considered and must be well understood.

Nowhere does the magic of Maya the preserver, life's fundamental law of illusion, deception, imagination, which holds all creatures in thrall— nowhere does it more show its deluding, teasing power than in love, in that tender craving of one single creature for another, which is so precisely the pattern and prime content of all the attachment, all the involvement and entanglement, all the delusions on which life feeds and by which it is lured to perpetuate itself. Not for nothing is lust, the love-god's most cunning mate, not in vain is that goddess called "gifted with Maya"; for she it is which makes any phenomenon charming and worthy of desire, or rather makes it seem so; the sense-element is contained in the very word "phenomenon," linking it with ideas of brilliance and beauty. Lust it was, the goddess and deceiver, made Sita's form so dazzling fair, so worship-ripe, to the youths at Durga's bathing-place, especially to the suggestible Shridaman. But note how glad and grateful the friends had been when the bather turned her head and they saw her face, that it was lovely too, little nose and lips, and brows and eyes; so that the sweet form had not been deprived of value and meaning by ugly features. We need only recall that to realize how much obsessed a man is, not only with the desired one but with desire itself; how he is not seeking sanity but intoxication and yearning,

and fears nothing more than to be undeluded, that is
to say relieved of his delusion.

And now see how this concern, that the little
phiz the friends were spying on might be pretty
too, proved dependence of the body, by its Maya-
meaning and value, upon the head to which it belongs! Rightly had Kamadamana, vanquisher of
desire, declared the head to be the highest of the
limbs and on that statement based his judgement.
Indeed, the head decides the value of the body for
love, and the impression it makes. It is not enough
to say that if it wore another head it would not be
the same. Let one single feature, one expressive
line be changed, and the whole is altered. Herein
lay the error which Sita in error committed. She
counted herself happy to have made it, because it
seemed to her paradisial—and perhaps in anticipa-
tion had appeared so—to possess the friend's body
in the sign of the husband's head. But she had not
forseen—nor in her happiness would at first admit
it—that the Nanda-body, when combined with the
narrow-nosed Shridaman-head, the thoughtful,
mild eyes and cheeks covered with soft fan-shaped
beard, was no longer Nanda's lively body but another one altogether.

Another it was, at once and from the first minute after his Maya. But not only of this do I speak.
For in time—the time that Sita and Shridaman
spent "at first" in perfect relish of their sensual joys,
in the incomparable delights of love—the body of
the friend, so hotly coveted and won at last (if one
may still so designate the body of Nanda in the
sign of Shridaman's head, when in actual fact the
far-away husband-body had become the friend-

body); in time, then, and indeed in no long time, the Nanda-body, crowned with the honoured husband-head, became of itself, and aside from any Maya, quite a different one. Under the influence of the head and the laws of the head, it gradually became like a husband-body.

That is the common lot, the regular effect of married life. Sita's melancholy experience differed on this point not greatly from that of another woman who presently no longer recognizes in her easy-going spouse the slender lusty youth who wooed her. Yet here the common lot had a special bearing and cause.

The Shridaman-head had proved its sway when Sita's wedded lord continued to dress his new body as he had the old and not as Nanda did. Again, he did not follow Nanda's practice of anointing his skin with mustard oil. His head could not tolerate this odour on his own person; he stopped using the oil and that was rather disappointing to Sita. Another slight disappointment was the fact that when Shridaman sat on the ground his posture—as need hardly be said—was conditioned not by his body but by his head. He had contempt for the rustic position beloved of Nanda, and sat sidewise as he always had. But all these were trifles and belonged to early days.

Shridaman, the Brahman's grandson, continued, even with Nanda's body, to be what he had been and to live as he had lived. He was no smith nor herd, but a vanija and son of a vanija, who helped his father carry on a respectable trade; as the father declined in strength the son took over the business. No heavy hammer did he wield, nor pasture the kine on the mountain Bright Peak; but bought and sold mull and camphor, silk and calico, likewise rice-mallets and firewood to supply the needs of the folk at Welfare of Cows. Between times he read in the Vedas. It was no miracle then, however miraculous the tale may otherwise sound, that Nanda's arms soon began to lose their strength and grow thinner; his chest to narrow and relax and some slight fat to gather on his little belly—in short that he fell more and more into the husband pattern. Even the lucky-calf lock failed him; not entirely, it merely grew thinner, so that it was scarcely recognizable as Krishna's sign—Sita his wife observed it with pain. It is undeniable that a certain refinement, in part Brahman, in part clerkly, an ennoblement, if you like, was—aside from any Maya—bound up with the change, and extended even to his complexion, which turned some shades lighter; his hands and feet grew smaller and finer, more delicate the bones and knee-joints. And in short the joyous friend-body, in its former life the chief of the whole, turned into a tame appendage to a head, into whose noble impulses it soon neither could nor would enter with any paradisial completeness, and even bore them company with a certain reluctance.

Such was Sita's and Shridaman's wedded experience, once the truly incomparable joys of the honeymoon were past. Things did not get so far that the Nanda-body changed back completely into the Shridaman-body—when indeed everything would have been as before. Our narrative will not exaggerate, rather it emphasizes the factors limiting the bodily change, and its restriction to unmistakable signs, in order to gain understanding for the fact that the effect was reciprocal between head and limbs; since the Shridaman-head, conditioning his I- and my-feeling, underwent adaptation in its turn. This might be explained on natural grounds by secretions common to head and body; but on philosophical ones by loftier considerations.

There is an intellectual beauty and one that speaks to the senses. Some people will have it that the beautiful belongs solely to the field of sense; they separate the intellectual entirely from it, so that our world presents a picture of cleavage between the two. This is the basis of the Vedic teaching: "Bliss experienced in all the universe is of two kinds only: the joys received through the body and those through the redeeming peace of the spirit." Yet it follows directly from the doctrine that the spirit does not stand in the same relation to the beautiful that the ugly does and is not inevitably one and the same. The things of the spirit and mind are not synonymous with the ugly, nor need they be; for they take on beauty through knowledge of the beautiful and love of it, and express that love as spiritual beauty. So their love is by no means an irrelevant and hopeless thing; for by the law of attraction of opposites the beautiful yearns in its turn towards the spiritual, admires it and welcomes its wooing. This world is not so made that spirit is fated to love only spirit, and beauty only beauty. Indeed the very contrast between the two points out, with a clarity at once intellectual and beautiful, that the world's goal is union between spirit and beauty, a bliss no longer divided but whole and consummate. This tale of ours is but an illustration of the failures and false starts attending the effort to reach the goal.

Shridaman, son of Bhavabhuti, had by mistake been given a beautiful, sturdy body to accompany his noble head, where love of the beautiful reigned. And his intelligent mind straightway found something sad in the fact that the strange had now become his and was no longer an object of admiration—in other words that he was now himself that after which he had yearned. This sadness unfortunately persisted throughout the changes which his head suffered in combination with the new body; for these changes were such as go on in a head that through possession of the beautiful more or less loses the love of it and therewith its own spiritual beauty.

The question remains open whether this process would not have taken place anyhow, without the bodily change, simply because Shridaman now possessed the lovely Sita. We have already said that the case in general was like the common run, though exaggerated and accentuated by the circumstances. To the objective listener, it is merely an interesting fact, but to the lovely Sita it must have been a distressing and sobering sight, that her husband's fine thin lips got fuller and thicker in his soft beard until they finally curled over in a roll of flesh; that his nose, once thin as a knife blade, took on fleshiness too, and showed an undeniable inclination to droop and decline into the goatlike. His eyes in time wore an expression of rather heavy joviality. The final product was a Shridaman with a finer Nanda-body and a coarser Shridaman-head; there was no longer anything right about him at all. And here the narrator would particularly invoke the sympathy of his hearers for Sita's feelings as she watched the changes and drew inevitable conclusions about corresponding changes which might have taken place in the distant friend.

She thought about her husband's body, which she had embraced in not precisely blissful but sanctified and provocative bridal night, and which she no longer possessed—or which, if you like, as it was now the friend-body, she still did not possess—and she doubted not where the lucky-calf lock was to be found. Moreover she definitely suspected that a refining process must have taken place in the loyal friend-head which now sat atop the husband-body, corresponding to the refinement of the friend-body now crowned by the husband-head. It was this speculation, even more than the other, that moved her. Soon she had no more rest by day or night, not even in her husband's moderated arms. The lonely and doubtless beautified husband-body hovered before her, wearing a pathetically refined Nanda-head, and suffering spiritually from the separation. Longing and pity for him so far away were born and grew in her, so that she closed her eyes in Shri-daman's wedded embraces and in lust waxed pale for very woe.

12

When her time was come, Sita bore to Shridaman the fruit of her womb, a little boy, to whom
they gave the name of Samadhi, which means "col-
lection." They waved a cow's tail above the new-
born to ward off evil, and put cow-dung on his
head to the same end—as was right and proper. The
joy of the parents (if that is the right word) was
very great, for the boy was neither pale nor blind.
True, he was very light-skinned; but that might
come from his mother's Kshatriya or warrior blood.
He turned out later to be very nearsighted. Thus
do prophecies and folklore get themselves fulfilled,
somewhat darkly and imperfectly. You may say
they have "come true," or that they have not, as
you like.

After a while Samadhi got the nickname of
Andhaka (little blind one) on account of his near-
sightedness, and the name gradually ousted the first
one. But the weakness lent his gazelle-like eyes a
soft appealing gloss and made them even lovelier
than Sita's, which they resembled. All in all, he
took far more after her than after either of his two
fathers, she was obviously the clearest and most un-
equivocal element in his composition, and it was
natural that his form should shape itself to hers. He
was pretty as a picture; and once he had got past
the stage of soiled and crippling swaddlings he
proved to be a model of symmetry and strength.
Shridaman loved him as his own flesh and blood; and

his soul began to register certain feelings of abdication, a desire to hand over the business of living to his son.

But the years in which Samadhi-Andhaka developed into loveliness at his mother's breast and in his hammock cradle were just the ones during which the changes slowly took place in Shridaman's head and limbs, turning his whole person so decisively into the husband-form that Sita could endure it no longer. She felt an overmastering sympathy with the far-off friend in whom she envisaged the begetter of her little son. The longing to see him again, to see what he in his turn might have become by operation of the law of correspondence; to show him his delightful offspring, that he too might have his joy in him, that longing filled her soul to overflowing, yet she dared not communicate it to her husband-head. So when Samadhi was four years old, and was called Andhaka more often than by his name; when he could run, but more often fell down, it happened that Shridaman went away on business, and Sita made up her mind, whatever the cost, to seek out Nanda the hermit to console him.

One morning in spring, by starlight and before the dawn, she put on her pilgrim shoes, took staff to hand and with the other clasped that of her little son, dressed in his shirt of cotton from Kalikat. With a sack of provisions on her back she stole away unseen, and by great good luck was soon off with him out of house and village.

Her intrepidity in face of the hardships and perils of her pilgrimage is evidence of the great urgency of her desire. Her warrior blood, watered down though it might be, may have come to her

aid; certainly her beauty did so, as well as that of
her son; for everybody rejoiced to help the lovely
pilgrim and her shining-eyed companion on their
way with word and deed. She told people that she
was journeying in search of her husband, father of
her child, who had felt irresistible craving to con-
template the nature of things and so had become
a forest hermit. She wished, she said, to conduct
her son hither, that his father might bless and instruct him; and this too made folk's hearts soft, rev-
erent, and gracious to her. In the villages and ham-
lets she got milk for her little one, almost always
she procured a night's lodging for herself and him
in hay-barns and on the earthern banks of furnaces.
Often the jute and rice farmers took her long dis-
tances in their carts, and when there was no such
conveyance, she paced onwards with her staff un-
daunted, in the dust of the highroads. She held
Andhaka's hand and he took two steps to one of hers
and with his shining eyes saw only a little space of
the road before him. But she saw far ahead into the
distance to be travelled, the goal of her pity and
yearning fixed before her eyes.

Thus in her wanderings she reached the Dankaka forest, having guessed that her friend had there
sought himself out an unpeopled void. But she
learned from the holy men she asked that he was
not there. Many could or would say nothing more;
but some good-hearted hermit-wives who had fed
and petted little Samadhi told her kindly where
Nanda was. For the world of the hermit is very like
other worlds: when you belong to it you know your
way about there, and all the gossip and jealousy and
rivalry and backbiting that go on. One hermit of

course knows where another hermit lives and what he is doing. So these good women could betray to Sita that Nanda the hermit had set up his rest near the river Gomati (the Cow River), seven days' journey distant by south and west. It was, they said, a spot to gladden the heart, with all kinds of trees, flowers, and clinging vines, full of bird-song and hosts of animals; the river-bank had roots, tubers, and fruits in plenty. All in all Nanda had chosen his retreat in almost too pleasant a spot, and the more austere among the saints did not take his asceticism very seriously, particularly as he observed no vows save bathing and silence, and ate the fruits of the forest as they came to hand, with wild rice in the rainy season and even now and then a roast bird. In short, he was merely contemplative after the fashion of any disappointed and dejected man. As for the way thither, it was without special difficulties or hardships, except for the robbers' pass, the gorge of tigers, and the vale of serpents, where certainly one needed to have a care and to take one's courage in both hands.

Thus instructed, Sita took leave of the friendly woman of the Dankaka and with fresh hopes continued her journey as before. She surmounted the difficulties each day as they came, and haply Kama the god of love, in bond with Shri-Lakshme, mistress of good fortune, guided her steps aright. Unassailed she put behind her the robbers' pass; the gorge of tigers she went round, by instruction from some friendly shepherds, and in the vale of serpents, which lay directly on her route, she carried little Samadhi-Andhaka the whole way in her arms.

But when she came to the Cow River she set

him down and led him by the hand, with the other
planting her staff. It was a morning shimmering
with dew. Awhile she paced onwards along the
flowery banks; then as she had been instructed
turned landwards across the plain to a strip of woods
behind which the sun was just rising. The blossoms
of the red ashoka and the kimshuka tree made the
woodland glow like fire. Her eyes were dazed by
the brilliant dawn; but when she shaded them with
her hand she distinguished a hut at the edge of the
clearing, thatched with straw and bark, and behind
it a youth in bast garments girdled with grasses,
working at the structure with an axe. As she drew
yet nearer she saw that his arms were strong like
those that had swung her up to the sun; but his nose
came down towards the only moderately thick lips
in a refined way that could by no stretch be called
goat-like.

"Nanda!" she cried, her heart on fire with joy.
He seemed to her like Krishna, who is overflowing
with the juices of great tenderness. "Nanda, look,
it is Sita coming to you."

He let fall his axe and ran towards her and on
his breast he had the lucky-calf lock. With a hundred welcomes and by a hundred pet names he spoke
to her, for he had yearned sorely for her in her
entirety, with body and soul. "Art thou come at
last," he cried, "thou mild moon, thou partridge-
eyed, thou all-round lovely-limbed, fair-hued thou,
Sita, my wife, with the glorious hips! How many
nights have I dreamed that you came so to the out-
cast and solitary across the wastes, and now it is
really you, and you have conquered the robbers'
pass, the tigers' gorge, and the serpents' vale, that

I wilfully put between us out of anger at the judgement of fate! Ah, what a splendid woman! And who is this you bring with you?"

"It is the fruit," she said, "that you gave me in first holy wedded night, when you were not yet Nanda."

"That will not have been much," said he. "What is he called?"

"He is named Samadhi," she replied, "but more and more he is called Andhaka."

"Why so?" he asked.

"Do not think he is blind," she responded. "He is no more blind than he is pale, despite his fair complexion. But he is truly very short-sighted, so that he can only see three paces before him."

"That has its good side," Nanda said. They set the boy a little distance from the hut, in the fresh green grass, and gave him flowers and nuts to play with. Thus he was busy; and what they played —fanned about with the mango-flower fragrance spring sends to heighten desire, and to the music of the kokils' trilling in the sunlit treetops—that lay outside the range of his vision.

❀ *13* ❀

The story goes on to tell that the wedded bliss
of these lovers lasted but a day and a night. The sun
had not risen for the second time above the fiery
blossoms of the wood beside Nanda's hut when
Shridaman came on the scene. He had known as
soon as he got back to his empty house whither it
was his wife had gone. His family at Welfare of
Cows had tremblingly announced the disappearance
of Sita, and had surely expected that his anger would
blaze up like a fire into which butter is cast. But
that did not happen; he had only nodded slowly
like a man who had known it all before. Nor had
he set out after his wife in wrath and lust for re-
venge; he went indeed without rest but also without haste, direct to Nanda's retreat, having long
known the precise spot and kept the knowledge
from Sita in order not to hasten fate.

Mildly, with drooping head, he came riding
on a yak; dismounted under the morning star before the hut, and did not even disturb the embraces
of the pair within, but sat and waited for day
to break them off. For his jealousy was of no ordinary kind such as is commonly suffered with furious
snortings by disseevered beings. It was lightened by
the knowledge that this was his former body with
which Sita was now renewing her marriage vows
—an act that might as well be called faithfulness as
the reverse. Shridaman's knowledge of the nature
of things taught him that it was in principle unim-

portant with whom Sita slept, with him or with his friend, since even though one of them had nothing from it, she always did it with both of them.

Hence his lack of haste on the journey and his patience and composure as he sat in front of the hut and awaited the dawning of day. But we shall see that notwithstanding he was not minded to let matters take their course. The story says that at the first ray of dawn, while little Andhaka still slept, Sita and Nanda came out of the hut with towels round their necks, to bathe in the near-by stream; thus they perceived the friend and husband, who sat with his back to them and did not turn round as they appeared. They came before him, greeted him with humility, and in the end wholly united their wills to his, recognizing as inevitable what he had excogitated on the way about their problem and its solution.

"Shridaman, my lord and honoured husband-head," said Sita as she bowed low before him, "greetings and hail—and believe not that your coming is unwelcome and awful to us. For where two of us are, the third will always be lacking; forgive me then, that I could not hold out longer with you but overcome by pity sought out the lonely friend-head."

"And the husband-body," answered Shridaman. "I forgive you. I forgive you too, Nanda, as on your side you may forgive me for acting on the judgement of the holy man and taking Sita for myself, only considering my own I- and my-feeling and not troubling about yours. You would have done just the same if the holy man's judgement had been in your favour. For in the madness and divisions of this life it is the lot of human beings to stand in one another's light, and in vain do the better-constituted long for an existence in which the laughter of one would not be the weeping of another. All too much have I insisted on my head, which rejoiced in your body. For with these somewhat diminished arms you swung Sita up to the sun and in our new distribution I flattered myself I had everything to offer for which she yearned. But love has to do with the whole. So I had to suffer that our Sita abode by your head and went out of my house. If I could now believe she would find her lasting joy and satisfaction in you, my friend, I would go my way and make my own retreat in the house of my fathers. But I do not believe it. Possessing the husband-head on the friend-body, she yearned for the friend-head on the husband-body. And just as certainly would she feel pity and sympathy for the husband-head on the friend-body, nor would she find any peace and satisfaction, the distant husband would ever be the friend whom she loves, to him would she bring our son Andhaka, because she sees the father in him. But with both of us she cannot live, since polyandry is not permitted among superior beings. Am I right, Sita, in what I say?"

"As thy word sayeth, so, alas, is it, my lord and friend," answered she. "My regret, however, which I sum up in the word 'alas,' refers only to part of your words, and has no reference to the abomination of polyandry, for I cannot regret that it does not come into consideration for a woman like me. Rather I am proud. From my father Sumantra's side some warrior blood still flows in my veins, and against anything so base as polyandry everything in me rises up. In all the weakness and wilderment of the flesh one has yet one's pride and honour as a superior being."

"I had not expected otherwise," answered Stridaman. "You may be sure that I have from the beginning taken into consideration this attitude, as distinct from your female feebleness. Since you cannot live with both of us, I am certain that this youth here, Nanda, my friend, with whom I exchanged heads, or bodies as you like, Nanda will agree with me that neither of us can live, and nothing remains but to put off the division we have exchanged and unite our essences once more with the All. For where the single essence has fallen into such conflict as in our case, it were best it melt in the flame of life as an offering of butter in the sacrificial fire."

"Most rightly, Shridaman, my brother," said Nanda, "do you count on my agreement with your words. It is unconditional. I should not know what we could still have to seek in the flesh, since both of us have gratified our desires and slept at Sita's side. My body could rejoice in her in the consciousness of your head and yours in the consciousness of mine, as she rejoiced in me in the sign of your head and in you in the sign of mine. But out honour may count as saved, for I have only betrayed your head with your body, and that is quitted, in a way, by the fact that Sita the lovely-hipped betrayed my head with your body. Brahma has preserved us from the worst; that I who once shared the betel-roll with you in sign of loyalty, should have betrayed you with her as Nanda in head and body both! But even so we cannot honourably go on like this, since we are too enlightened for polyandry and promiscuity;

certainly Sita is, and so are you, even when you have
my body; and I myself too, now that I have yours.
Therefore I unreservedly agree with everything
you say about mingling our essence. Here are these
arms, they have been strengthened in the wilderness, I offer them to build the funeral pyre. You
know I have already offered before. You know too
that I was always resolved not to outlive you, and I
followed you without hesitation into death when
you sacrificed yourself to the goddess. I only betrayed you when my husband-body gave me a certain right and Sita brought me the little Samadhi,
whose bodily father I must consider myself, though
I willingly and respectfully concede your parent-
hood according to the head."

"Where is Andhaka?" asked Shridaman.

"He is lying in the hut," answered Sita, "col-
lecting in sleep strength and beauty for his older
days. It is time we spoke of him; for his future ought
to be more important to us than the question of how
we shall come with honour out of all these perplex-
ities. But his case and ours are closely related, and
we shall be acting for his honour in acting for ours.
Were I to stay behind with him, as I might,
I suppose, when you withdraw into the All, then
he would pass through life as a wretched orphan
child forsaken of honour and joy. Only if I follow
the example of those noble Satis who united themselves to the bodies of their dead husbands, and
mounted with them into the fire, and monuments,
stone tablets and obelisks were erected to their memory on the place of their burning—only if I leave
him will his life be honourable and the favour of
men fall upon him. Therefore I, the daughter of

Sumantra, demand that Nanda build the funeral pyre for three. As I have shared the couch of life with you both, so shall also death's fiery bed unite us three. For after all, on the other we were always three."

"Never," said Shridaman, "would I expect anything else from you; for from the first I have known your high spirit and your pride, and that they dwell in you along with the weakness of the flesh. In the name of our son I thank you for your resolve. But we must consider well how to rescue our honour and human pride out of the desolation into which the flesh has brought us. We must take great care for the form that rescue takes; and in this particular my thoughts and plans as I have developed them on the way hither differ somewhat from yours. The high-hearted widow turns herself to ashes beside her dead husband. But you are not a widow as long as one of us is alive; and it is a question whether you would become a widow by sitting living with us in the fire and dying as we died. To make you a widow Nanda and I must kill ourselves, I mean we must each kill the other; in our case either is right and both come to the same thing. We must fight like bucks for the doe; I have provided two swords, they hang on the girth of my yak. But it may not be that one shall win and survive and carry off the fine-hipped Sita for himself. That would do no good, for ever would the dead man be the friend after whom she would consume herself with longing, till she paled away in her husband's arms. No, we must both fall, each struck to the heart by the other's sword—for only the sword is the 'other's,' not the heart. That will be better than if each of us turned the sword against his own present division; for it seems to me our heads have no right to decree death to the body attached to each, any more than our bodies had the right to wedded bliss wearing heads that do not belong to them. Indeed the battle will be sore; for the head and body of each of us must take care not to fight for itself and the possession of Sita, but to remember the double duty of giving and receiving the mortal blow. Still, each of us brought himself to cut off his own head—and this mutual suicide cannot be harder than that."

"Bring on the swords," cried Nanda. "I am ready for the fray, and find it is a just solution to our rivalry. It is just, because in the process of adaptation of our bodies to our heads, our arms have come to be of almost equal strength—yours stronger on my body, mine weaker on yours. Gladly will I offer my heart to your weapon. But yours I will pierce through that Sita may not pale for love of me in your arms, but doubly widowed join us in the flames."

Sita professed herself satisfied with these arrangements, she said they appealed to her warrior blood. Wherefore she would not withdraw from the combat but look on unflinching. So then this mortal meeting took place forthwith in front of the hut where Andhaka lay asleep, on the flowery mead between the Cow River and the red-blossoming woodland; and both young men sank down into the flowers, each pierced through the other's heart. Their funeral, because of the religious ceremonial of suttee combined with it, became a great festival. Thousands gathered on the place of burning to watch the little Samadhi, called Andhaka. As next of kin male he brought his near-sighted gaze to bear and laid the torch to the pyre built of mango and sweet-smelling knots of sandalwood, the interstices filled with dry straw soaked in melted butter that it might catch quickly. Within the pyre Sita of Bison-bull had found her place between her husband and her friend. The pile blazed heavenwards to a most unusual height; and if the lovely Sita shrieked awhile—because fire when one is not already dead is frightfully painful—her voice was drowned out by the yelling of conches and rolling of drums so that it was just as though she had not shrieked. But the story says, and we would believe it, that the heat was cool to her in the joy of being united with her twain beloved.

An obelisk was set up on the spot in memory of her sacrifice, and what was not entirely burnt of the bones of the three was collected, drenched with milk and honey, and buried in an earthen pot which was thrown into the holy Ganges.

But the little fruit of her womb, Samadhi, who was soon called nothing but Andhaka, he prospered upon earth. Famous through the feast of the burning, he enjoyed favour as the son of a monument-widow, and to that was added a love called forth by his increasing beauty. Even at twelve years old he was like an incarnation of a Gandharva for charm and supple strength; and on his breast the lucky-calf lock began to show. His poor eyesight, far from being a handicap, kept him from living too much in the body's concerns and directed his head towards the things of the mind. A wise and learned Brahman took charge of the seven-year-old lad, and taught him right and cultured speech, grammar, astronomy, and the art of thought. At the youthful age of twenty he was already reader to the King of Benares. On a splendid palace terrace he sat, in fine garments, under a white silk umbrella, and read aloud to that prince in a pleasing voice, from the sacred and profane writings, holding his book close in front of his shining eyes.

THOMAS MANN was born in Germany in 1875 and died in Switzerland in 1955. He was awarded the Nobel Prize for Literature in 1929, and left Germany for good in 1933. Among his major novels are *Buddenbrooks* (1901), *The Magic Mountain* (1924), the tetralogy *Joseph and His Brothers* (1933, 1934, 1936, 1943), and *Doctor Faustus* (1948). He is equally well known for his short stories and essays, both of which are available in collected editions. Mann's *Last Essays* was published in 1959.

THE TEXT of this book was set on the Linotype in a face called Janson, an excellent example of the influential and sturdy Dutch types that prevailed in England prior to the development by William Caslon of his own designs, which he evolved from these Dutch faces. Of Janson himself little is known, except that he was a practising typefounder in Leipzig during the years 1660–1687. This book was composed, printed, and bound by THE COLONIAL PRESS INC., *Clinton, Massachusetts. Paper manufactured by* S. D. WARREN COMPANY. *Cover design by* PAUL RAND.

Vintage Books